Predator Cop

By

Carl Crozier

Predator Cop

Carl Crozier

ISBN-10: 0-9977051-6-7
ISBN-13: 978-0-9977051-6-4

Library of Congress Control Number: 2018901316

Printed in the United States of America.

BELLA JOHNS ENTERPRISES
PUBLISHER

INTRODUCTION

It's an acknowledged fact that there are police officers that have taken advantage of their position of authority to put the lives of citizens that they are sworn to protect, in jeopardy. Some officers have committed transgressions against their populace which include beatings, arrest, incarceration, theft and even death. For the most part, those officers have committed those wrongs with impunity against the Black community. Most citizen complaints in the Black community, against officers, are either ignored or dismissed. Some are never even recorded. White citizens have a better chance of having a complaint investigated then do Black people. Also, the number of complaints against police officers in the White communities are much lower than in areas that are mostly Black. Police officers who service White areas do not violate their authority to the extent that they do in the Black community.

Some officers join the police force and bring to the job undetected backgrounds that are not compatible with police work: such as racist tendencies, bullying, sexism, deviant behavior and a penchant to committee economic crimes.

The character in PREDATOR COP is one such officer. This officer, who has had a lifetime of undetected predation before he joined the police force, continues his unethical and unlawful behavior after becoming a police officer. Unlike many officers, who never answer for their transgressions, this officer meets justice –meted out after he becomes the prey of one of his former targets.

• • •

PART I

In the wild animal world there are predators and there is prey. Lions are predators. Zebra are one of their preys. Killer Whales prey on seals and cheetahs run down their prey, which are mostly antelope. Predation is practiced by animals in order that they are able to survive. The wolf will not live unless he captures, kills and eats buffalo, beer or other carnivores. Most predators are fast, or they have endurance. They run down their prey with a burst of speed or they continue the chase until the prey can no longer flee from their pursuers. Many animals use a combination of speed, endurance and cunning to capture their prey. The hyena is mostly a scavenging animal, getting their nourishment either stealing from other predators, who have killed the prey, or eating after the prey has died a natural death. Hyena have been seen nonchalantly walking among prey as if they have no interest in capturing a meal. The prey is lulled into a false sense of not having to be on guard when all of a sudden the hyena will pounce and cunningly kill to obtain their meal.

Humans are also predators. Although, for the most part, with the exception of primitive societies, humans do not have to hunt for their sustenance. Humans can be thought of as cunning creatures in the procurement of their quarry. They domesticate their animals and then kill and eat them. Cattle, sheep, chickens and pigs are raised and fattened for slaughter and then distributed by a few to the many. Fish are the only prey that is still hunted at sea but recently fish farms have sprouted up around civilized man. The supply of food for humans is left to specialized groups or corporation for the profit of those specialized groups. Humans, unlike most animals, do not hunt their victims for food one-on-one. Unless, they are doing it for their own pleasure or sport.

• • •

Although humans have surpassed the need to individually practice predation of animals for food they have not lost the ability of being predators for other purposes. Humans carry out predation practices on other humans that they consider weaker or less intelligent in areas that the predator feels superior. Nowadays, humans practice predation mostly for power, money or sex. Many human predators operate in the financial realm. There are predators that have the financial capacity to lend money to less fortunate individuals who for whatever reason are in dire need of cash. The predator charges exorbitant interest rates to those who can least afford the 'juice'. Other financial predators devise plans to sucker their prey out of the prey's money on bogus investments commonly known as Ponzi schemes.

Another example of predation practiced by humans is the exploitation of labor. Capitalists or the owners of the means of producing commodities have preyed on the labor of others to produce their products. They exhort workers (the prey) to labor at wages that are set by the industrialist predicators - "work at our wages or starve to death." The capitalist is concerned with their profits. The worker be dammed! History is full of examples of the struggles between capital and labor. Remember slavery? Labor was only able to thwart capitalist predation by organizing unions. If it were not for unions or the threat of unionized labor, many would still be preyed upon by the rich who own the means of production.

Human predators abound in our world. Society is full of them. The thug that sticks a gun in the old lady's belly and takes her purse is a predator. The teacher that seduces a fifteen-year-old boy is a pedophile predator. The daughter that is sodomized by her step father has been preyed upon by a predator. The preacher who uses monies collected from his congregation to sustain a lavish lifestyle - preyed on his flock. The power hunger politician schemes and lies to his constituents to retain his office and stuff his pockets full of cash. He's a smooth predator.

Human predation doesn't occur in the abstract or in theory. There are faces of individual predators who are practitioners seeking human victims to prey upon, for whatever reason. Let's meet one. His name is Drew Harrison. He's a cop. At this stage in his life, Drew is 30 years old.

Drew was raised by his grandmother along with two other siblings. His momma gave up her kids to her mother to rise after each was born. The children's mother was a part time whore and when she got too old for whoring she became a full-time booster – stealing from department stores. She was good at her trades but even the good people get caught sometimes. She did a couple of stints in the county jail – both for prostitution and stealing. When she could, she came over to her mother's house and gave her mother money to help with the kids. She also stayed there sometimes when the streets got too hot for her and she needed a cooling out period. She had a drug habit - so most of her cash went for drugs for her and her pimp. She never had a lot of money to give. Drew had a brother and a sister. None of them favored each other. They all were the result of the mother's whoring – trick babies.

The grandmother, like all Black grandmothers who have to be responsible for their daughter's or son's children, did the best that she could in raising the kids. She had legal custody of them – therefore she received public aid, food stamps and medical care for her daughter's babies. Besides taking care of their physical needs, she tried to instill them with values but it's hard to have values when you are poor. If you have to lie to some welfare agency to get extra benefits for yourself and the children, she would do it. She was religious to an extent but if she had to bend values to put food on the table or clothes on their back, she would bend those values and rationalize that Jesus would understand. Children were not meant to go without if you could help it. She avoided welfare fraud charges about additional income because she was never caught lying about additional monies that she received as a domestic worker.

Drew was the oldest of the brood. He was two years older than his sister, who was one year older then her younger brother. Through their pre-teens, the kids led a pretty ordinary life - like many poor ghetto children. They lived in public housing. They matriculated through the public grammar schools that really didn't care about whether they learned or not. Their grandmother was no help in seeing that they got a good education. She only went to the 10th grade before she had her first child and was on public aid at 16. She encouraged her grand kids to get an education, but she was unable to intellectually help them. Her grandchildren participated in the government breakfast program to save the grandmother money and they all learned to live and survive on the tough streets on the south side of Chicago.

The early teen years, were the years that the children developed the personalities that would define them for life. At thirteen Drew's sister's body came into flower like a grown woman. She was enticed by a pimp and she ran away from home. He put her on the street and she followed her mother into the oldest profession. Drew's brother was a juvenile delinquent at twelve years old. He and a couple of other young neighborhood kids formed a purse snatching, bike stealing, burglarizing fraternity. He was a bully to his peers. He wasn't that smart though. He

would get caught time and again and the system finally
determined that grandmother couldn't control him. He was in and
out of reform school during his teenage years.

Drew was a loner. He never fit in with the kids his own age. He
was smart and good looking. He had an abnormal interest in
woman and sex. When he was eleven he engaged in peeping at
naked grown woman. The housing project that he lived in
consisted of two story row houses. There were two bedrooms on
the top floor and one bed room on the ground floor of each
cookie cutter row house. The ground floor bed room was in the
rear of the house. There were 10 houses to a row in the complex.
It was a very large development with over 20 10-row buildings.
One evening, just when it was getting dark, Drew was playing
ball by himself in the back of one of the buildings. He was about
eleven years old at the time. As he went to retrieve his ball that
had settled against the building wall, He happened to look into an
open screened window with the shade slightly up. An older
woman was in the room in the process of taking her clothes off.
Drew froze. It wasn't the first time that Drew had seen an
unclothed woman. He had seen his mother and other woman that
she sometimes brought to the house naked when his mother came
to visit. Her visits were a respite in that she would show up when
she needed a break from her street life. She would come home,
get a good meal, take a bath and crash naked in his sister's room.
He was drawn to look at her naked body as she slept and feel
some excitement as he looked. There was never a mother /son
relationship between the two of them. But looking into the
window, at this woman, gave his mind a more intense pleasure.
He pressed his body tightly against the wall so that he could look
sideways into the room, without the woman seeing him. The
woman was oblivious to him. She rubbed her body as she
undressed, not sexually but as a woman would do to relieve the

stress of having on a tight-fitting brazier and griddle. She was a big woman, not obese but a woman with ample body parts. Large breasts hung from her chest. Her behind protruded into that roundness that black woman are known for and her thighs were thick as they rose to the crevice of her pubic hair. As he looked at her he began to rub his crouch and his penis felt like it would burst through his pants. The more he looked the harder he rubbed. The pleasure was so good that he wanted to cry out – but before he knew it, it felt like he had wet his pants and the feeling of intense pleasure that he had experienced ebbed away. He had had his first climax. At that moment, he became hooked on looking at naked women. He became a voyeur.

Over the next years, as a teenager, one of Drew's main forms of entertainment was peeping through windows to see naked ladies. But during those years he also developed his main form of entertainment: screwing as many girls and older women – mostly older women – as he could. His first actual sexual encounter occurred as a result of working one of the many hustles that contributed to his economic well-being. He cut grass, shoveled snow, delivered papers and carried groceries home for women who did not have a car to transport what they had bought at the local super mart. As stated before, he was tall, handsome and looked older than his thirteen years. One Saturday, he had hung around all day at the super mart carrying groceries home for women. It was late, and the day was turning to darkness. He had just about made the amount of money that would last him for the upcoming week. He decided to stay for another half an hour to see if he could add a couple of more dollars to his take. A woman approached him and asked if he would carry her packages. He most often had to ask the ladies to carry groceries, so it was a little odd that he was being asked but all that he could think of was here was another dollar to be made. The lady did not have a lot of groceries, but the couple took off with Drew carrying the packages. They walked about four blocks from the store when the lady turned into a pathway that led past a house. She headed for a garage. Drew thought that there must be an apartment over the garage in which she lived. When they got to the back of the garage they were in the alley that ran the length of the block. The lady stopped and faced Drew "You ever had a woman?" she asked. She took the packages that Drew was carrying and put them on the ground. She straightened up and her hand darted to Drew's crotch. Drew being caught completed off guard could not supply an answer. Drew was getting excited and he was squirming. The woman took Drew's hand with her other hand and guided it under her dress. She did not have on underwear and Drew felt the coarseness of the hair on her vagina. He also felt the moistness in the inside of that organ as she thrust his hand inside of her. She now had his attention. She kissed him, unzipped his pants and pulled his penis out. She played with it until it was hard.

By the time of this occurrence, Drew had had a lot of experience looking at naked women through windows, but he had no experience with actual intercourse. At this stage, in his peeping tom experiences, he had seen a man and woman having intercourse, but he had rather see the woman alone so that he could view the naked body. Drew was a loner and he had limited contact with boys of his own age. He would rather be engaged in earning money and in his voyeur obsession then to establish camaraderie with the fellows. The boys his age thought that he was a little strange, but they did not fuck with him because he was bigger than most of them and had previously proved his ability to fight. Had he established normal boyhood friendships, he would have known all about sexual intercourse because that was a topic that was discussed among boys in his age group.

• • •

The woman in the back of the garage lay down on the ground and pulled Drew on top of her. She had to guide his penis into her genital. He instinctively began to thrust and after four or five thrusts he emptied sperm from his body into her. After he completed the act, he jumped to his feet. He had experienced climax through masturbation, but this was the first time ejaculation was experienced with a partner. He felt a sense of not knowing what to do – if anything – next. The woman was not through with him. She had not gotten the sexual satisfaction that she had sought. She tried to hold on to his legs urging him to continue the act, but he was through with her. He pulled up his pants, ran and left her lying on the ground.

In the years that followed, he always looked back on his first sexual encounter and felt a sense of guilt in that he did not satisfy the woman that took his virginity. She must have been hard up for sex in that she turned to a boy for gratification. In that recollection, he figured that she was a late twenties or early thirties woman. When she kissed him, he could smell alcohol on her breath. The encounter left him with a taste for women that drank. He liked to fuck women who were boozed up. After the incident he never encountered the lady again in life. He kept an eye out for her but never saw her again. She disappeared into the urban jungle.

As his high school years progressed, Drew, unlike his brother and sister did go to and stay in school. He turned out to be a little better than an average student. In his environment, it didn't take a whole lot of effort to be better than average. He liked to read and reading helped him attain passing grades. His instinct also told him that he could have a better future if he stayed in school. He dabbled in playing a little basketball as the other kids his age did, but basketball did not hold any interest for him as it did the other boys his age. His interest was sex. The girls liked him for his good looks and his cool. Many wanted to have a girlfriend-boyfriend relationship with him. He wasn't interested in a relationship. He wanted their sex and that was all. He developed cunning ways of getting what he wanted from some girls - but mainly from older woman. He schemed his way into ladies' affection.

As a teen, Drew worked a number of part time jobs. This being the only way that he could secure any honest income. His Grandma could not give him any steady spending money. He had jobs such as a delivery boy for an Arab-owned food store in the neighborhood, a stock boy in a grocery store and he also worked in other fast food joints. During his teenage years, he mowed lawns in the summer and shoveled snow in the winter. All of his jobs brought him in contact with women older than himself. By the time he was fifteen, he had developed a cool, smooth persona which he always used with the opposite sex. His persona which included being a very mannerable young man, along with his near six-foot chiseled body frame, his dark smooth black skin, his piercing eyes, sharp facial features and naturally curly hair made him attractive to females both old and young. He probably had mixed Indian and Black genes but because he never knew who his father was, his ancestry would remain a mystery.

He learned to flirt – in a subtle way – with most women that he met, and many would flirt back with him. He developed an instinct for spotting woman who were vulnerable in one way or the other. He sized up most every woman that he met – both young and old – as being a potential victim for his desire. "What would they be like to fuck?" was the question that he always asked himself. He had more success with older woman than he had with girls his own age. Older woman knew what they wanted and were not shy about being receptive to his advances. Especially, if they were boozers.

 At fifteen, he had had a lot of conquests; a typical conquest would be like the Ms. Johnson conquest. He met Ms. Johnson on one of his jobs. She was a woman of 45 to 50 years of age. Well he really didn't just meet her at that time. He knew her when he was eight years old. Ms. Johnson was a white woman who lived in the neighborhood. She had a Black child and Drew's grandmother used to watch her child while Ms. Johnson worked. The kid was Drew's age and they played together when the boy was staying at his house. Ms. Johnson and the kid's father were not together. At Some point, Drew knew the boy's father took custody of the kid and moved to Kansas City, Kansas, when the boy and Drew were about 10. Drew did not see Ms. Johnson again until he saw her come into the Arab store that he was working at. It was about five years after her kid had went to Kansas City with the father. At first, she did not recognize Drew. He had done a lot of growing in those ensuing years. Once she recollected who he was, she showered him with compliments. "My, you sure have grown up to be a fine looking young man," she said. "How is your grandmother? Give her my regards and tell her that I said that she raised a handsome young man." Drew, as always, exhibited good manners with the woman but as they talked he couldn't help noticing that the woman seemed slightly inebriated and she had a couple ½ pints of gin in her basket. Drew remembered that his grandmother used to say that the woman drank too much, and he began wondering about the woman's sex as they stood talking. He didn't obsess about her as he never did about any woman. If it was meant to be, it would happen. He could not put the woman out of mind because she was regular at the store and she was very friendly with the owner. Each time she came in, she would strike up a conversation with

Drew and she would heap compliments on him. Drew took them in stride. but he did not make any overt advancement toward her.

One day, the owner called Drew in the office and told him that Ms. Johnson had called and wanted the owner to see if Drew would drop a package off to her house after work. She would pay him for the effort. Drew agreed to the delivery and after work the owner gave drew the package to deliver. It consisted of two half pints of gin. Drew walked the three blocks to the woman's apartment. She lived in a court way complex in a middle-class section of the neighborhood in which the Arab store was located.

Drew's public housing project was about 8 blocks (a mile) away from where Ms. Johnson lived. Drew found her entrance and rang her bell. She inquired "whose there" over the intercom and Drew identified himself. Her apartment was on the second floor and Drew bounded up the stairs. She was at the open door when he arrived on the 2nd floor landing. She was bare footed wearing a bathrobe as she ushered him into her apartment. Drew was impressed with two things. Most of her body was visible through the partially closed robe and her apartment was very clean, orderly and well furnished. Drew knew from the time that he was a little kid that Ms. Johnson had a good job at the telephone company.

A good portion of her breast was exposed, and Drew envisioned that he could see her private parts even though they were not clearly visible. Drew recognized that the woman was drunk as she slurred her speech while she attempted to thank him for bringing her package. She gave Drew a hug. Drew's heart began to beat fast. He was aroused. It came to him – he was going to fuck this white woman now.

Ms. Johnson was a tall slender woman with skinny legs, a flat ass and large breasts. At a little past middle-age she was not a beauty but rather homely looking. Drew determined that he needed an excuse to stay. He asked Ms. Johnson if it was alright to use the bathroom "Yeah sure "she said as she pointed him in the direction of the facilities and as she also began opening one of the half pints of gin that Drew had delivered. Drew lingered in the bath room after he urinated. He was buying time trying to figure out what to do next. When he emerged from the toilet he moved down the hall, but he did not see Ms. Johnson. As he came back to the parlor area he could see that she had moved to the living room which was to the left of the front door. She was sitting on the living room couch and as she saw Drew come into view she beckoned to him. She had money in her hand – intending to pay him for the delivery. As Drew approached the couch he noticed that the television, which was in front of the couch, was on. Drew faked excitement about the program that was on TV. Stating that "this is my favorite program. Would you mind if I stayed and watched it?" he asked. "Sure, sure," Ms. Johnson replied, "make yourself comfortable."

Drew sat on the floor in front of the couch. He was aware that Ms. Johnson was half sitting-half lying on the couch. She was drinking from the bottle of gin without a glass as he sat down in front of her. For the next ½ hour or so Drew forged phony interest in the TV program. He and Ms. Johnson had slight conversation about the program details, but he could sense that Ms. Johnson was continuing to drink and was slipping away in a drunken stupor. Drew did not turn around to look at Ms. Johnson. His eyes were focused on the television - his mind was focused on Ms. Johnson. But he did not want to turn around and look at her or to continue conversing with her because he felt that if he looked too soon he would alert her to his planned undertaking.

He watched another program during which he did not hear Ms. Johnson stir. At the end of that program he slightly turned his head and viewed that his perseverance had paid off. Ms. Johnson was flat laid out on the couch. One leg resting on the couch proper and the other leg slung over the side, resting on the floor. Her robe was open and the complete front of her naked body was viewable. Drew got up and went to stand over the prostrate body lying on the couch. He stared at her for a few minutes. He was feeling accomplishment in that his plan to fuck her had worked. She had a pouch for a stomach and the hairs on her pussy were straight not kinky like Black woman. Her breasts were large, but they sagged almost to her belly button. She had a chin that almost disappeared into her neck. This was the first naked white woman that Drew had seen. He bent down and softly touched her breast to make sure that she was in a deep drunk sleep. She did not respond to his touch. She continued to snore lightly. Next, Drew lightly kissed Ms. Johnson's nipples and smelled her private parts. He had been introduced to oral sex, but he did not want to do it on this occasion because Ms. Johnson's body aroma was not inductive to him putting his head between her legs.

Drew began to take his clothes off and to exercise his penis. It was good and hard enough already. Drew spit on it to ensure lubrication. His heart beat fast in anticipation of the pleasure that he was about to receive. He thought better then to lie on top of the woman to penetrate her. He just wanted to slide his penis into her privates without putting pressure on her body. Pressure might wake her up before he started the intercourse. He didn't care if she woke up after he was in. The way that she was laying on the couch was helpful. One leg was flat on the couch; the other leg was hanging over the sofa. Her foot was touching the floor. All Drew had to do was to move that leg slightly and the path to her canal should be open. Drew moved the leg, scooted down and tried to penetrate her. She was dry. Normally, Drew could have forced the penetration, but he was still leery of applying pressure to her body that might wake her up before he really got started. He was going to finish fucking her. He withdrew his penis and began to think about what he could use to lubricate his organ. He was well endowed, and he had learned that spit would not always work. His favorite lubrication was baby oil, but he had not come prepared. He walked around Ms. Johnson's apartment until he located her bedroom. He spotted a bottle of lotion on her dresser along with some loose currency. He decided that the lotion would have to do. He took the lotion and a small amount of the bills and went back to the living room. He hurriedly stuffed the money into his pants that were lying on the floor and returned to the business at hand – trying to fuck Ms. Johnson.

He put an ample amount of lotion on his penis and then gently rubbed an amount on to the colitis of Ms. Johnson. He attempted penetration for a second time and with a slight amount of pressure, he was in. He did not thrust right away. He looked at Ms. Johnson to see if she reacted to his incursion; the old girl didn't budge. He had just wanted to get off and leave but for some reason he prolonged the occurrence. He would softly plunge just to the point of ejaculation then stop, rest and start over again. He stretched the fuck out for about ½ hour – amazed that Ms. Johnson did not wake up. He almost wanted her to wake up. He finally decided to end his dalliance and he ejaculated on her stomach. He had developed the practice of releasing sperm on the woman's body when he had sex with girls his own age in order to prevent their pregnancies.

After finishing, Drew was glad that Ms. Johnson didn't wake up. He decided that it was best to get the hell out of there as quick as he could. Drew put his clothes on, put Ms. Johnson's legs on the couch, covered her with her robe and left the apartment.

Drew had more such encounters with older woman throughout his teenage years. Although, alcohol was involved with these women, they were not quite as drunk as Ms. Johnson. There was an old – once good looking – prostitute who was a rummy and a drug addict that was still trying to turn tricks. Drew had seen her on a number of occasions but once when Drew saw her and determined that she was really strung out he approached her and offered to turn a trick with her. She followed Drew into an abandoned building on the promise of getting paid. Once in the building, Drew gave her the money, laid her on the floor and pulled off her pants and panties. He made her take off her bra, saying that he needed to suck her tidies in order to get his dick hard. Drew unzipped his pants and plunged into her. This was just a quick fuck for Drew. He came in the whore's mouth. When finished Drew got up and zipped his pants. He was ready to leave. The old girl couldn't leave that quickly and Drew had counted on that. She had to put back on all of those cloths that Drew had taken off. As she attempted to dress, Drew snatched his money back and fled the building. The last he heard, as he exited the building, was the lady calling him all kinds of pussy mother fuckers.

The few young girls his own age that Drew screwed were border line consensual/rapes. As stated before there were many young girls who wanted to have a relationship with Drew. Drew was a clean cut, good looking young man who had no problem establishing connections with young women when he wanted to, and if he determined that the girl would be vulnerable to his intentions. Drew paid attention to girls that no one else wanted. Ugly, homely, passive minded, slightly fat young females were weak to his sexual advances. Drew felt that pussy was pussy. An ugly girl had the same thing between her legs that a good-looking girl had. But she was usually much less resistant to his sexual advances. Unattractive girls were starved for male interest and felt incredulous when someone as good looking as Drew showed interest in them. Drew never took them out or dated them in the traditional sense of a date. He might walk one home or sit with a girl that he had targeted at lunch – in school. The closest that he would come to dating was to have the girl meet him in a secluded place. Drew wasted little time with dating etiquette. He would have his hands up the girl's pants as quick as he could arrange to get the girl in a compromising position. They usually coyly resisted his advances saying such things as "stop I'm a virgin." Drew had no problem with overpowering them to get to their goodies – always at the same time playing mind games with them. Telling them "baby I love you" while he continued to tear away the little resistance that they offered. He took their body and climaxed on their stomach to prevent impregnating them. After each conquest, Drew would spend time – right then and there – mind fucking the girl to impress her that they had just done a beautiful thing. He didn't want her to go away and cry rape. He would spend as much time as necessary to brain wash the young girls into believing that they had performed an act of love that would bind them to a future. After that, the girl would be lucky if he paid any serious attention to her when she next saw him. "Hi, how you doing?" he might mutter. But he didn't have much more conversation with the young lady after that.

Drew Harrison was a sexual predator, but he was not one dimensional. As his teenage years progressed he began to be affected by the world around him – even though his world was limited. His world was limited to the ghetto but even in the ghetto there were some positive role models that made Drew think about his future. Drew wanted to be prosperous. He could easily see that the acquisition of money was one of the keys to prosperity and to a good life. There was one key legitimate role model in Drew's life. Drew had a great uncle – his grandmother's brother – who had a very successful life. He and his wife were both school teachers. They lived in the suburbs of Chicago. They liked Drew and often had Drew come to their house for dinner. Drew was very impressed with their home and the life that they led. Their house was large, and it was well furnished and immaculately kept. Unlike the house he lived in with broken down furniture, paint peeling off the walls and torn carpeting. The housing authority that managed the property that he lived in was totally neglectful and would only commit to repairs infrequently.

Drew's great uncle, besides being a teacher, was a real estate agent. During Drew's high school years, the uncle would hire Drew to help clean up property that the uncle had acquired through tax sales. The uncle led a very successful life because of his legal economic achievements. Drew was impressed with this relative and listened to the advice that was freely given on many occasions when the two were together. "Stay in school, work as long as you can, don't do drugs and stay away from gang involvement" were some of the counsels given to Drew by his great uncle.

As Drew became older, he became more acutely aware of his surroundings and was able to think about the environment that his life was being shaped in. As a teenager he could see what was happening in his little world of the ghetto, but he was not able to understand the forces that produced what he saw. He was impressed with people who had things – cars clothes, nice living surroundings. He was impressed with signs of prosperity.

He knew that money was the fuel of life that drove the engine but there were very few Black people who were driving the train. There was a minute number of Black owned business in his community. The barber and beauty shops seemed to be the most numerous Black owned establishments. The grocery stores, wig shops, liquor stores, currency exchanges, fast food joints, car repairs and gas stations were not Black owned. As far as he could see the Arabs, Jews and Koreans owned those establishments. Some cleaners were owned by Blacks and then there were the taverns on some blocks which catered to the people in the community. Naturally, they were Black owned.

There were other people in the community that appeared to be financially well off and Drew knew that those people had "good" jobs. They were school teachers, municipal bus drivers, garbage workers, policeman, fireman, factory workers, insurance salespeople and people who worked downtown. Drew was not sure what the downtown workers did.

All of the people with "good jobs" appeared to have a pretty good life as compared to the people who lived in the poverty public housing environment that Drew was trapped in. The people with the "good" jobs had homes, nice apartments, newer model cars, better clothes and on the whole, they seemed to have a better life.

There was one aspect that puzzled Drew as a teenager. Why could some people make it – have more things – then others and lead a better life? As he grew in his teenage years he came to the understand – not all at once – that establishing goals, being persistent, acquiring knowledge, accumulating money and having luck were the majority of the keys to a better life.

Drew certainly had luck (but he didn't realize it) because he persisted with his voyeurism obsession throughout his teenage years. He had developed ten or fifteen windows where he consistently visited to peep at his ladies. One of his windows was wedged at the junction of two three story buildings that were almost – but not – joined together. The buildings met or almost met at an angle. One of the buildings overlapped the other slightly. The woman's bedroom in which he was peeping was shielded by the protruding other building. Drew had stashed a milk carton in the alley at this location and he fetched this carton every time he visited the window to stand on – so that he could just see into the window. The woman had blinds on her window, but they were bent at the bottom, so they could not properly close. The bent blinds left just enough opening for Drew to see inside the room without been seen by the lady. Drew's milk carton (which he stood on) elevated him to a height that allowed his eyes to peer just over the window sill of the first-floor apartment.

The light in the bedroom went on like clockwork at about 9:00 PM every night. Drew figured that she was just getting home from work at that time. This was Drew's favorite lady to look at. The woman, who looked to be in her fifties, went through a ritual every night. She was fully clothed when she came into the room. Her hair was rolled in a bun and she loosened the bun and let her salt and pepper shoulder length hair fall down her back. She combed her hair and then began to undress. The stockings came off first. Then followed by the skirt, a slip and then her top were removed in that order. Her panties and bra remained on while she hung up her clothing. She was a big, shapely, olive skinned woman, not overly attractive in the face but also not ugly. She looked like she weighed about 180 to 200 pounds with broad shoulders. She was about 5 feet 8 inches. The woman appeared to be a stern, no nonsense woman. He imaged her to be a church going lady like the woman he had seen when his grandmother had forced him to go to church when he was a young boy. He never saw her smile. He would have liked to fuck her to see if her demure would change but he knew that it would never happen.

Her panties could not hold all of her enormous buttocks. Her butt overflowed her panties at the bottom and her breast spilled out of the top of her brassiere. For Drew, it was like a strip tease act. He always began pounding his penis when he saw her parading around in her underwear. When she was ready to liberate her massive breasts from her bra and free her butt from the constraints of her panties, Drew was ready to climax – and he would – upon seeing her completely nude. She would walk around nude in her room doing other things for a short time after that. Drew would try to get it up again as he watched her move around the room, but his organ would not produce the sperm again so quickly. She would then turn off the light and disappear into another part of her apartment. Drew surmised that she would then go to take a shower or bath. The whole episode took about 15 minutes and Drew always made sure that when he did show up at her window he would be on time to see the whole show.

From time to time, Drew would explore other parts of the neighborhood trying to find new windows to peep into. He would walk down alleys trying to spot potential windows for his excitement. One night he was in an alley and he saw the lights coming from a first-floor window in a building which was about 50 feet from the alleyway. Drew reasoned that the window should be a bedroom because of its placement. He had to enter the building's back yard through a gate that was aligned with the building's garage. The gate was closed but not locked. He opened the gate and went through the back yard until he reached the building with the window. Drew had to grab hold of the window sill and pull himself up in order to see into the room. The light was on but there was no one in the room. It was indeed a bedroom. Drew lingered at the location for a short period of time and decided to move on when there was no activity in the room.

Drew did not go back into the alley to exit the location but climbed the 3-foot fence into the yard of the next building. Drew continued to climb fences into different yards looking to see if he could spot other lighted first floor windows. As he climbed one fence and landed on the ground, Drew happened to look back and saw a light dancing on buildings in the direction that he had left. He froze wondering what was the source of the light. Drew crept to the edge of the fence in the yard that he was in and looked down the alley. He made out a car moving slowly down the alley projecting the light that had caught his attention. It was a cop car. As the car came closer to his location, Drew's first impulse was to run. He bolted for the fence to the next yard, but a realization came to him that he could not run his way out of his predicament. Drew dropped to the ground, became motionless and tried to become one with the dirt and grass in that yard. In a few seconds the cop car was at his location and the light was shining on the building of the yard in which he was in. The cop was shining the light at the first-floor level. The light did not scan the ground. The cop car moved on to the next location leaving Drew on the ground with his heart pounding and an urge to piss his pants. Drew stayed in his position hugging the ground for about ½ hour. He did not hear the cop car come back down the alley. When he figured that the cop had gone on to the next block he proceeded to get up and crawl to the rear gate of the back yard that he was in. He exited the yard and crept down the alley in the opposite direction in which the police car went. He left the alley and took various streets until he felt safe in that he was out of that neighborhood.

After he got back home and calmed down. His heart rate – which had zoomed – returned to normal and he was back in the safety of his own room. He asked himself questions about what had just happened. Do cops routinely patrol alleys looking for peeping toms? It took him some time to figure out what happened, but later when he was older he surmised that someone had seen him in the alley and called the police. They probably though that he was a burglar. After that incident he rarely went looking for new places in strange neighborhoods to get his thrills. He stuck fast with his proven locations to get his voyeurism excitement. He had plenty of proven windows to look into. He only came close to being caught as a voyeur one other time.

Drew's life as a teenager moved on. All his teen years he continued his deviant behavior. He was in awe by the different Black body types that he saw by looking into the widows of naked women. Skinny women with hardly no breast. Skinny women with large breast. Bulbous fat women with stomachs so large that he would have had to be able to lift their stomachs to see their vaginal parts. Women with humongous asses that left little room as they passed through the doorway of their room. Women with wiggle waggle arms and bulges over their bodies. Drop dead fine women with asses, legs and thighs that looked so good it left him drooling. Old women with breasts sagging to their waist. Young women with bodies that were in different stages of development. Masculine looking women with broad shoulders like football players and tight asses. Short stumpy women. Tall Amazon women. The women that he saw nude were all hues from jet black to high yellow, looking like they were white. Drew reveled in looking at the female form. He enjoyed them all. Now, on occasions, he caught his victims in the act of sex, both homosexually and heterosexually. He climaxed when that happened.

He continued to be a loner among his peers. He never developed friendships. He knew that his interests were different than other boys his age. He didn't have any problem with the gang bangers in the hood. By the time he was seventeen, he was six feet three inches and he weighed 220 lbs., which helped keep the neighborhood punks out of his face. It didn't make him immune to violence because the punks didn't care how big you were. A .38-caliber pistol was always an equalizer and the punks were well armed. But he was cool toward the gang boys that ran the street and they were cool to him. They had tried to recruit him when he was a shorty but after he turned them down and put an ass whipping on one of the lower level gang members, they left him alone. "What's happening" would be exchanged by Drew and any of the gang boys as they passed on the street.

Drew went to and stayed in school. He almost never cut classes in high school. He was by no means a Rhodes Scholar, but he completed his assignments and managed to get C's and occasional B's on his work. The influence of his great uncle and the uncle's prodding for him to graduate from high school kept him focused on accomplishing that objective. His mannerism in the classes was quiet and his teachers liked him. They thought that if he would open up he could be a student leader and possibly influence other kids. Various teachers sometimes approached him to become active in student affairs but after they became aware of his disinterest in interaction with others, they left him alone. He continued to use his cunning to pick off vulnerable girls for his sexual pleasure. Those girls were just sex objects and he developed no emotional feeling toward them. His only contact with them after sex was to convince them to leave him alone.

He could write better than most. He had no problem putting sentences or paragraphs together and he once or twice contributed articles for the school newspaper. He never caused any problems in school. After four years he was ready to graduate, and his graduation was a cause for celebration in the family. The grandmother and the mother had not graduated from high school. Sister and brother would not graduate from high school. Drew was the first in the immediate family to earn a high school diploma. All the family and the extended family attended the graduation with the exception of his younger brother who was still in reform school. The great uncle who had encouraged Drew to stay in school came through with a $500 graduation present. An extremely proud mother and grandmother beamed as he went across the stage to receive his diploma. His baby sister and her pimp also attended the ceremony.

From all appearances, Drew was such an upstanding young man. He worked. He went to school and he was never caught by the law doing his thing. No one in the family had any idea of his deviant behavior.

After graduation, Drew was faced with the same dilemma that confronts many a teen at that point in their life. What was he to do with the rest of his life? Drew had to get on with the business of securing a livelihood. He needed a serious job. Working at odd jobs was not going to cut it forever. If he continued to work as a stock boy in a grocery store or cutting grass or shoveling snow or working at fast food joints he would be in his grandmother's house for the rest of his life. He had to figure out how to leave. He wanted his own apartment, a car, clothes and other things that would make him an independent man. He knew what he wanted in life in terms of material things, but he was fuzzy about how he should go about getting them. He was not attracted to selling dope. That was a gang thing and he had stayed away from that environment throughout his high school years. He needed a job that would pay him enough to acquire the things that he wanted. The high school that he attended did not prepare him for a vocation. At the time of his graduation from high school, college was not on his radar screen. His great uncle kept insisting that he enroll in a community college, but continuing schooling was not in Drew's plans. He was not motivated for higher education. He flirted with the idea of joining the Army but decided against that.

While he continued to work at a neighborhood supermarket as a stock boy he applied for jobs at factories, retail stores, temporary agencies, better class restaurants (he had heard that waiters in those restaurants made tips that were good enough to live on) and county and city jobs. After six months of applying he did not get one reply from the applications that he had submitted. Then he got lucky.

A shopper came into the supermarket where Drew worked as a stock person and approached him. He was a regular customer. Drew had seen him often over the years, but he had not ever had a serious conversation with the man. Drew remembered that he had answered the man's question from time to time concerning where certain items were. He greeted Drew. "How you do?" he asked. "Ok," answered Drew. "The store manager told me you graduated from high school," he said. "Yeah," replied Drew. The man continued, "my name is Clyde Keaton. I own a pest control business and I am looking for a couple of dependable young men because I just got a city contract to help get rid of rats. Do you think that you would be interested in taking a job that deals with rats and other disgusting pests?" "How much does it pay?" asked Drew. Keaton replied, "The job would start at $10.50 per hour and if you work out, the pay would increase to $13.50 per hour after 6 months. Drew didn't have to calculate. He was making $8.50 per hour. He would welcome the chance to make more money. Drew said, "yeah, I'm interested."

Mr. Keaton told Drew that he had heard from the store manager and had seen from his own observation, as a customer, that Drew was a reliable employee. He indicated that he needed reliable people in his business He related to Drew that he had three main criteria for his workers. They had to perform the job they were responsible for. They had to be on time for work and they also had not to be absent. Keaton told Drew to give the store manager his notice and to report to his office in two weeks at 8 o'clock sharp.

On the appointed date, Drew reported as directed. After filling out the appropriate paper work, he began his training with Mr. Keaton and other company employees. Riding in company trucks, they patrolled the allies of the company's territories in the part of the city that the business was assigned. They put down poisonous bait for rats and set traps for other animals that are considered pests in the city. Mr. Keaton exposed Drew to every phase of the business which included getting pests out of garages, crawl spaces, chimneys and attics. Some of the work was dirty and a little dangerous if you didn't handle the critters carefully, or if you didn't learn how to walk on slanted roofs, you could be seriously injured.

During training, Mr. Keaton saw to it that Drew got his driver's license because after training, Drew would be responsible to drive a company truck, cover part of the territory assigned to the company and service customer calls on his own. Drew loved the job, He didn't mind getting dirty or crawling in crawl spaces or climbing roofs to get critters that were making their homes in customers' attics. The twenty-year-old felt that he was lucky to have a man's job with what he considered to be decent pay for one so young. The average kid in his neighborhood didn't have a job and if they had a job they were making minimum wage.

Drew's day involved him in picking up his truck and supplies. He got his schedule and he was off to perform his tasks of laying down poison and baits in the alleys, picking up dead rats which had succumbed to bait laid down at earlier times. He made house calls to customers that had called about pests in their homes. His training had taught him to deal with bees, roaches, raccoons and just about every other critter considered despicable by homeowners or renters.

Drew's job was legitimate but it also gave him a greater opportunity to indulge in his darker side. He was still a voyeur. As he worked at his job he was able to scope out targets for his night time activities. He was in the city alleys everyday baiting traps and removing dead rodents. As he worked he looked for and identified homes and apartment buildings where he could peep at his unsuspecting prey. He found properties where it would be safe to exercise his habit. He eliminated spots that he determined would be dangerous to indulge his criminal endeavor. Places with dogs or residences that were wide open with no other buildings to offer cover were eliminated as targets.

Although his work took him into Black, White and Hispanic areas of the city, he limited his criminal activity to the black areas. He rightly figured that he was less likely to raise suspension if seen after dark in African American areas of the city. His reconnaissance developed numerous sites for him to view his unsuspecting live actors for his erotic pleasure. His favorite site to peer into was a rundown coach house in the back of a dilapidated dwelling in a depressed neighborhood. The occupants in the house, up front, were a number of women with a lot of kids. The residents of the coach house were a black and white couple. The man was an old, weather beaten, pot belly, tired looking and unkempt Black man. His woman was a tall, boney, middle age, White woman who looked like she could have been the poster child for the American Cancer Society's campaign against smoking and cancer. She was a hag who looked like she was on death's doorstep. She constantly was smoking and coughing. Drew was drawn to see this couple on many a Friday night because of the show that they always put on.

The couch house had a car port on which no car had parked for quite some time. The car port was overgrown with weeds and with thrown away household items that were meant for the trash man but never made it further then the car port. The couple's bed room could be looked into from the car port. Drew would creep along the side of the house to the bedroom window and kneel down to look inside and watch the unintended show that was put on by the couple.

The couple was heavy drinkers and the woman was a drug user. Marijuana and cocaine were supplied for the woman by the man. The man would consistently demean the woman. Calling her "bitch, whore". He would slap her around, grab her by the throat and force her to suck his dick (as if she needed forcing). He would push her away and she would beg for more drugs. He gave them to her - a little at a time. He controlled her intake of the substances. After a few rounds of the same, he would strip the clothes from the woman and throw her on the bed face down and attempt to have intercourse with his woman from the rear. He would have a hard time trying to penetrate her – he couldn't get it up. His cursing and swearing would increase as his frustration mounted and he would physically abuse her – but never to a point to cause her serious harm. The woman would complain saying such things like, "I can't even enjoy a good fuck in peace." After a while the man would let up and another round of drinking, drugging, sucking and debasing would continue. The man would attempt intercourse at numerous times until he finally got an erection and was able to complete the act. Drew's arousal and climax would coincide with the culmination of the man's act. After climaxing the man did a complete turnaround. He treated the woman with love and tenderness. He cuddled the woman in his arms and said sweet things to her. He stroked her hair and rubbed her back. At that point, Drew would wipe his member with the tissues that he carried and quietly exit the scene. Drew spent countless hours over a period of time viewing these less then handsome couples and their sexual escapades. He peeked at other couples and their sexual interactions and copulations, but none were as bazaar as the couple in the coach house.

Although, Drew continued to involve himself in his dereliction, he also developed for himself some one-on-one relationships with females of his choice. His choices were older women. During the course of performing his job duties he encountered a number of his type of females. One such person was Mary, a sixty-nine-year-old well-preserved woman. She was an attractive woman whose face showed her age, but her body contradicted father time.

He met Mary when she called his company and ordered services to eliminate the termites that had nested in the southeast portion of her house. Drew was assigned to eliminate Mary's problem.

● ● ●

By the time Drew came to work on Mary' house he was a well experienced exterminator. He made the necessary trips to Mary's house to rid her of her pest problem.

Mary was a three-year widow without the means of much social interaction. When alive, her husband had sheltered her from interfacing with those other than her children and his and her family. Her grown children had moved out of the area and family members that were left had health problems which limited the amount of time and occasions that she could communicate with them. Mary had a penchant for conversation. She loved to talk. Through the years of her marriage her husband accommodated her need to converse but isolated her from neighbors and other would be friends.

From the beginning of Drew's encounter with Mary, she talked. She shadowed him while he was performing his exterminator duties-and she talked. She invited him into the house for coffee- and she talked. Drew while not paying particular attention to what she was saying, faked listing. At intervals he would say "Uh huh" as if he was agreeing and understanding her. Drew was sizing her up and coming to the conclusion that Mary might be a good fuck but he didn't want to make a move on her because he had the good sense to understand that Mary was a customer of the company.

Mary indicated to Drew that she had some odd jobs to be performed around the house and that she was looking to engage someone to perform those jobs. The jobs consisted of mainly painting and replacing some tiles in her bath room. Drew agreed to take on the jobs in his spare hours. Each time that Drew was over Mary's house, she rattled on. Drew began to test how much she would allow him to put his hands on her body. He first hugged her upon departing after he finished a portion of the work that she had him involved in. The next time, he hugged her and held her hand as he left the house. Mary would prattle on. Mary talked with her hands from time to time during her conversation she would touch Drew's body. Her touch excited him. The next time he was over and after he finished his work, he hugged her and kissed her on the cheek -No objection came from Mary. Mary even returned the hug. During subsequent visits, the kiss on the cheek graduated to a rubbing on the back and a pat on the behind. Lastly, Drew's hand made it inside her house coat - cupping her breasts - again Mary raised no objections and went passively along as Drew placed her on the kitchen table and performed oral sex on her before he rammed his penis into her body. The 69-year-old and the twenty-one-year old were intimate after that – whenever Drew wanted it.

Drew had a number of older women whom he had met during the course of performing his work whom he had occasional sex with. He was satisfied with those relationships because he didn't have to worry about the woman falling giddily in love with him, or becoming pregnant and he didn't have to spend any money on them. They seemed tickled to death with him coming over and fucking them and they all enticed him over by providing him with a meal.

At this stage in his life Drew was satisfied with the way his life was going. He had a job and enough money to live on. He was still living with his grandmother and paying a small amount of his income to her for rent. He expected to get his own apartment in time but there was no hurry. He was saving his money until he could pay cash for the apartment's furnishing. He had bought a used car to go back and forth to work. Drew was a lot more conservative than his contemporaries. He dressed differently than other young men his age. No jeans. Dress pants were pressed, and he wore no pants hanging below his butt. He preferred short and long sleeve dress or polo shirts. No tees with logos were purchased by him. Older neighborhood folks referred to him as the clean-cut kid. They had no idea of his nighttime exploits. He was lucky enough to not have had any run-in with the law, although his deviate peeping behavior could have had him arrested on numerous occasions.

Drew knew a little more about Chicago then most young black men his age. His exterminator work took him into many parts of the city. There were Black areas, White areas (Polish-Italian-Irish- Jews) and Hispanic neighborhoods. The city was ethnically divided. His boss, who was Black, had warned him when he hired Drew to be careful when working in white areas. "Do your work and get out," he had said to Drew. As he worked, he observed how other races lived. There were some White and Hispanic areas as poor as most Black areas on the south and west sides of the City. But there were few if any Black areas that could match the many economically affluent white areas of the metropolis. Drew was impressed with those areas but at the time he had no idea of how to acquire the wealth to achieve a life style that would match what he was seeing in those prosperous areas. He did know that you could acquire wealth by dealing dope, but he had stayed away from that criminal activity all of his life and he wasn't about to start now. Besides, Drew was a loner and being involved in the drug trade meant involvement with a gang crew and Drew wanted as little involvement with other people as was necessary to achieve his own gratification. He grudgingly had relationships with his family because they were present in his life. By the time he was 22, his brother and sister had left the house. His brother was in jail on a robbery charge. His sister was living with her man who was her pimp. His mother was back at home. She had lost her looks, gotten fat and was now too old to whore. She took care of old people for the State. He had his best relationship with his grandmother who was very proud of him because he had a steady job and had not ever given her any problem.

Drew knew little of the world outside of his environment. He sometimes listened to the news on television and rarely read the newspaper other than the sports section. He was a baseball fan of the Chicago White Sox and from time to time he went to a ball game. He had never traveled outside of the Chicago Metropolitan area. His prospective on how the world affected him was minimal. Although he had graduated from high school, that level of education had not sparked a thirst for knowledge beyond survival and satisfying his primitive wants. All that was about to change, as a result of an incident that happened one day as he performed his work.

Drew received an assignment to eliminate termites from a home. During a search of the premise to determine where the termites were nesting Drew decided that he had to investigate the crawl space under the house. The crawl space was high enough to allow Drew to crawl along slowly under the length of the house. While looking for the termites, Drew came across a bone sticking out of the ground. Drew dug down with his hand beneath the surface where he found the bone and discovered more bones. He didn't know what to make of the bones, but he brought out a few of them and showed them to the home owner. The owner recognized them as human bones and called the police.

The police and detectives came to the house and began an investigation. The cops determined, preliminarily, that the bones were human. The lead detective, who took charge of the investigation, was Black. He aggressively directed his force of police officers in securing what he called a crime scene. He questioned Drew about his discovery of the bones and quickly determined that Drew had no involvement in the affair. In the end it was determined after lab analysis that the bones had been there for many years. The bones had been there longer than the present property owner had lived in the house. The corpse was ruled to have been shot because bullets were found in the torso that was eventually dug up.

Drew was completely impressed by the Black cop who led the investigation. He had interacted with cops before. but he had never seen a black in charge as this officer was. After being interviewed by the office he stood around and watched as the team of cops was directed by their leader. The cop instantly became Drew's role model. He determined that he wanted to be a cop. His heart was fired with ambition to become a police officer.

After the incident, Drew began to research on what it took to be a police officer. He found out that there were three factors that would qualify a person to be considered to become a cop. One needed to have 2 years of college, pass a civil service examination and not have a criminal record. Drew had never been interested in furthering his education but now he became obsessed with the idea of going to school. He conferred with his great uncle about going to college. His uncle recommended that he apply to a community college. The two-year college would be perfect for what he wanted to accomplish. He didn't want to be an intellectual. He just wanted the sufficient amount of credits that were required for his purpose. He consulted a college advisor at the community college in his area and at the next opportunity he enrolled, taking one course in the evening. As time progressed, he increased his enrollment to two evening courses.

He calculated that it would take 4 years, going to school at night to accumulate enough credits to get a 2-year degree. He recognized that he couldn't stop working, so he would become a part time student. In 4 years he would be 26 years old. His great uncle told him that 26 would be a good age to become a cop.

Once he got started in college, his motivation was not to become a scholar. He just wanted to qualify to take the police exam. If he got grades of all C's, that was fine with him. He put out just enough effort to pass his courses. During his 4 years, going to college Drew cut down on his voyeur engrossment. He was conscious of the fact that if he got caught as a peeping tom, his dream of becoming a cop would go out the window, but he couldn't break the habit altogether. Occasionally, he would look in on the couple in the coach house and he discovered other spots to view unsuspecting women, which he deemed full-proof from detection.

Drew was now old enough to do the bar scene. He acquired a taste for alcohol and became a moderate drinker. He would drink only in the bars, never at home. He was enthralled by the atmosphere in the lounges with the ambiance, the dancing, the crowds the crazy individuals and the music. He visited the bars not to do a lot of socializing. Unlike other young persons, he was not interested in hooking up. His enjoyment came from watching the interaction of the patrons whether they were dancing, posturing or trying to make out. When he first started going to the bars, he was hit on by the ladies. He was tall and handsome, but the regulars soon learned that no matter how they flipped and flirted with him, he was not interested. Drew was content with getting his sex from the old women that he had cultivated. He did not want any emotional involvement with the young ladies.

One day, Drew got a job assignment to perform extermination services on a three-flat building next to one of the bars that he frequented. It was an apartment building that had an ant infestation. After performing the indoor inspection, Drew moved outside because he knew that the ants had to have a starting point on the exterior of the structure. While outside of the building, Drew noticed that the back of the bar that he sometimes visited was a mere 10 to 20 feet from the building that he was performing the extermination services. The buildings ran parallel to the street and there was a six-foot fence between the two buildings as they extended to the street. The bar building had an indentation about half way through the length of its structure. The indentation was sort of V shaped. Drew walked over to the bar building which was a one-story structure to see what was in the indentation. Drew learned that on each side of the indentation there was a window with bars. Drew peered into the windows and saw that he was looking down into the bar's men's and women's latrine. One washroom on each side of the indentation. When one walked into the indentation you could not be seen from the street or from the building next door. Drew became excited about his prospects of peering into the women's washroom without having to worry about being seen doing it.

That night, Drew visited the bar. The bar was a popular night spot in that neighborhood. The establishment had a capacity to hold between 75 to 100 patrons. On certain nights, if you didn't get in before 10:00 PM, you couldn't get in. The patrons were a cross section of people who lived in the neighborhood. The bar's reputation of being a place where raucous fun could be had, also attracted people from outside the immediate vicinity. Young, middle aged and older patrons (mainly older men attracted by the younger women) frequented the bar. The bar had a disk jockey and a dance floor that stayed fully occupied with the young and middle-aged customers. The older men sat, drank, postured and ogled the young woman on the dance floor as they danced and gyrated to the blues and the rock and roll played by the DJ. The older men let it be known that they had money to spend on the younger women.

Drew entered the bar and sat for a while. He bought a drink and sipped it for a couple of hours. About the time that the bar was heavy with activity, Drew slipped out and made it down to the alleyway on the block. He walked the alley until he came to the opening between the bar and the building next to it. Drew walked the path between the bar and the building next door until he came to the indentation that he had located previously. He looked around to ensure himself that he would not be seen and he slipped into the indentation and went straight to the window that looked down into the women's restroom.

In this bar's toilet, the woman did more than eliminate bodily waste. Drew's vantage point allowed him to look into the women's stalls from above and also look over the stalls unto the floor of the lavatory where the sink and mirrors were located. It was a feast for his perverted eyes. Drew watched the woman defecate and urinate. He also experienced them changing, adjusting and removing their undergarments – for whatever reasons. Cannabis was bought, sold and smoked and other hard drugs were ingested and injected in the facility. Women did a lot of throwing up as a way of eliminating the stomach contents that had over indulged too much alcohol or drugs. The stalls were a place where lesbian love took place and some ladies would occasionally take a man into the stalls to buy drugs or to have sex – either oral or intercourse – for love, lust or money. Women who frequented the club knew that 'anything' goes in the women's washroom. Women clientele displayed no sense of shock when they experienced other women displaying weird, out of place behavior in the facility.

Drew visited the indentation in the building that housed the bar on several occasions. Each trip helped him to satisfy his compulsion to spy on women for sexual gratification. One night he had had his fill of his voyeur fetishism and he determined to leave "his" secrete place. He walked to the entrance of the indentation and turned the corner to proceed down the path when he saw the outline of a figure walking down the passageway. He quickly jumped back into the indentation. His heart rate accelerated. He whispered softly to himself "Did the person see me?" His mind raced, and his body became warm. His brain told him that he was in big trouble. He asked himself "Who the fuck was this person? What was his business back here? Was he a cop?" His thoughts began to process what could he do to avoid a confrontation with this individual. He went to the edge of the opening and he peered around the corner again. He could see the figure more clearly now. It was a man and he was still coming towards Drew's position. His first instinct was to run. If he ran in the opposite direction from which the man came, he would have to run to the street which ran in front of the buildings. He remembered that there was a fence at the front of the pathway. He would have to climb the fence and land on the sidewalk on the street. It was a busy street. No telling who would be on the other side of the fence and see him jump down from the barrier.

He had to solve his dilemma quickly. The man would be on his position instantaneously. His prospects would be dashed for becoming a cop if caught. He glanced down and saw some concrete ruble beneath his feet. He reached down and picked up a piece of the material. He positioned himself at the edge of the entrance and waited. He could now hear the footsteps of the man who was approaching. As the man came to the entrance and turned the corner to come into the indentation, Drew swung and hit the man in the face with the piece of concrete. The man went down. In the same motion that he swung, Drew was out onto the path and running in the direction from whence the man came. Drew did not look back. He did not know how much damage he had done to the man nor did he care. He only knew that he was not being pursued. He exited the alley onto the street. Everything seemed normal. The street was full of people but there was no cop car to be seen.

When he reached the street, his outward appearance was cool and calm. He made a motion like he was zipping up his pants. If anybody was looking, he wanted them to think that he was exiting the alley after peeing. Although he appeared calm, his mind was raging, and he was at war with himself. He had to walk a little further than a block to get to his car. It was the longest block in his life. He passed people on the way to his car and did everything that he could to present a nonchalant, cool and calm appearance. His outward appearance was in stark contrast to the rage that was going on within his body. He had a weird feeling that started in his gut and it rose to his throat. It left him dry as if something had sucked all of the fluids from his body. When he reached his car, he entered it and sat for a moment. "Stupid, stupid, stupid," he muttered to himself as he sat in the car. He banged his head against the steering wheel as thoughts about what had just happened raced through his mind. He kept up the conversation with himself. "Who was that motherfucker? Did he see my face before I hit him?" he asked himself. He continued talking to himself asking himself the one question that he could not answer. How bad did he hurt the guy? Finally, he realized that he needed to get out of the vicinity. He started his car and drove off.

When Drew got home, he continued to fixate on the evening's event. He tried to analyze what happened and why it happened. Why it had happened was easy. He recognized that his perversion had got him into a situation which had put him in jeopardy of his career aspirations. He didn't care about the health of the man that he had hit. He did hope that he hadn't killed him. If he was dead, there would be a police investigation into a murder. Even at Drew's age, he knew that the aggressiveness of the investigation would depend upon who the guy was. Drew figured that his chance of being discovered was minimal, but Drew hoped that the guy was just hurt and that the best thing that would happen would be that the guy would get up and walk away and maybe not even report an assault. After all, what was this dude doing back there in the first place?

In the ensuing days nothing happened. There was no news of a murder happening in that neighborhood. Drew did not go back to the bar – ever. Drew figured that he had dodged a bullet and he swore off of his obsession for spying at windows on unsuspecting quarry. He would intensify his preying on older vulnerable woman for sex. After all, that was not a crime. In order to satisfy his predator instincts, he stepped up his game for attracting and luring senior females. Besides preying on older woman whom he met in his job as an exterminator, Drew upped his skill as a handy man. He got numerous referrals from customer for jobs cleaning gutters, unstopping clogged plumbing pipes, trimming trees and other handy man tasks. He would only take jobs that where connected to older females who lived alone. Therein he was successful in his quest to add to his collection of conquests. All he had to do was to be mannerable, suave and at the right time, move in and sexually triumph over his prey.

During the next two years Drew's life was relatively uneventful.

• • •

He worked, He attended school. He did his share of going to bars and lounges. He did not cultivate any serious friendships with the exception of his older women who satisfied his sexual needs. He kept 4 to 5 ladies on a string at any given time. He did talk with cops he met as he performed his job responsibilities as an exterminator. The cops that worked in the neighborhoods that he serviced came to know him. He let it be known to them that his career goal was to join the force. His main inquiry of them was to ask questions about the civil service exam that he had to eventually take. Those that could remember gave him broad topics that were covered on the exam.

He still lived at home with his grandmother and his mother who had moved back in to her mother's house. His attendance at the community college was steady. He continually accumulated the needed courses toward the Associate of Arts, two-year degree. Everybody who knew him was proud of him. He was thought of as a young Black man, who stayed out of trouble, had a job (he wasn't pushing dope) and he was going to school. Very few people in the neighborhood knew that his career aspiration was to become a cop. He was also lucky enough to keep his dark side of voyeurism covered.

The Civil Service Exam to become a policeman was not given every year. It hadn't been given in a number of years. As Drew was approaching his final semester toward receiving his Associates Degree, the announcement came. The exam was to be given. Drew applied to take the exam. He took the exam and passed it with a score that placed him high on the list to be called for the policeman position. He also had to go before the Civil Service Board to take an oral exam. He aced the oral exam. Drew had now passed all of the requirements necessary to become a policeman.

• • •

The reason the City gave the exam was because there was a shortage of police officers. Retirement had reduced the number of cops. It was the intension of the City to begin the hiring process after the results of the examination were finalized. The City selected 100 men and woman that had passed the examination to enter the police training facility. Drew was one of those selected.

Drew entered the Police Academy. The academy's primary purpose was to prepare the cadets for a career in law enforcement. The length of training was for 6 months. Much of the training occurred in the classroom. The cadets were trained in the law, human relations and report writing. The training also covered arrest, booking procedures, preliminary investigation procedures, defensive driving, pursuit policies, firearms training and physical training. The training was rigorous and some of the cadets did not make it. Drew was not one of those that didn't make it. He graduated from the academy with his proud family in attendance at the ceremony.

Upon graduation Drew was assigned to a precinct on Chicago's South Side. The citizenry was mostly Black. Rookies are partnered with veteran officers in order that they learn true policing methods. Methods learned on the job might vary somewhat from the training that they received in the police academy. His veteran partner was white and appeared to Drew to be a good cop who knew what he was doing. Assaults, robberies, murders, gang violence, domestic violence, traffic violations, drug trafficking and prostitution were crimes committed by the citizenry that Drew was obliged to police. His veteran partner was a straight-laced cop who was on the verge of retirement and while he was partnered with Drew, he saw to it that Drew did not deviate from applying proper policing – according to the law.

Upon becoming a police officer, Drew felt a sense of self respect for himself. He didn't necessarily feel that most people in the community respected him in his role as a police officer. Drew's motivation for policing was not the "serve and protect" motto that is advertised by so many police departments. He had been a loner all of his life. His dictum was a selfish one. He wanted to do what he had to do so that that he could survive and take care of himself – not so much different than anyone else. In the beginning of his career, Drew followed police procedures to the utmost as he performed his duties. He was a courteous, professional officer who was conscious to be mindful of the fact that the population he was servicing was not always enamored by the police because of the negative reputation that the police had with the community. In the community that Drew worked, people had mixed feelings about the police. When a citizen needed a police officer because they were the victim of a crime, they wanted the police to be there but otherwise many people thought of policemen as a despicable lot because of past transgressions committed by the police on the community. The vast majority of police in Chicago who patrolled the area where Black people live were white. Many Black people looked at the police force as occupiers in their community.

Police officers are subject to come into contact with situations that could be a temptation for corruption. Money and sex are the two biggest factors that are confronted by police officers that lend themselves to potential corruption. Cops are often offered money to look the other way when they come upon violations of the law and some cops find ways to get money themselves by engaging in illegal activity such as robbing drug dealers or burglary. Sex is not only offered to cops, but cops sometimes solicited sex from violators or victims of crime.

• • •

Drew's debut as a police officer into unethical practices was not something that he had planned. It occurred because of him performing his duties in a domestic violence case. Drew and his partner answered a domestic violence call. The perpetrator, who was the male, had put a whipping on the female and the officers had to subdue and arrest the man after he put up a pretty good struggle. Drew did the heavy work in subduing the offender and while his partner took the offender to the squad car and called the arrest in to the precinct, Drew had to get a statement from the victim. Drew was intent on doing his job to get the statement, but the victim was intent on making a pass at Drew. Drew finally got the statement after he promised to call the victim at a later time. By the time they got the man back to the station – booked and jailed – their shift was over. Drew started to go home when he remembered the victim and the phone number that he had in his pocket. He agonized a little bit because he knew that it would be unscrupulous to contact the woman. He surmised that a contact would lead to sex with the victim. After tossing it around in his mind, the predator that he was came to the forefront. Here was a weak human being that he could take advantage off – he made the call. The woman asked him to come over. He did and before the night was over they had sex.

That encounter was the first of a number of victims and lawbreakers whom Drew came upon in the line of duty who presented occasions to be involved in unprincipled behavior. Drew had crossed the line with his first crime victim and over the next few years he took advantage of his position of authority to prey on vulnerable female petty criminals whom he stopped for possession of drugs, driving without a license, drunk driving and prostitution. Drew developed a sense to determine whom, among the female law breakers that he encountered, could safely be preyed upon and taken advantage of for sex. The women whom he busted and begged him for a break were the most likely to fall victim to his predation. From the start of his dereliction of values of a principled police officer, Drew felt no pangs of guilt for his actions. He rationalized his behavior in that he came to feel that he was giving his victims a break in that they were guilty of breaking the law or committing a crime. He was saving them from the stress and hardship of being arrested and being processed through the criminal justice system. He was the policeman, the judge and the jury for his victims. For those that he picked to give a break and have sex with, he generally had sex in the squad car. He knew all of the secluded spots in his area of patrol where he could park his squad car and be unobserved and undisturbed.

Drew was careful in picking his victims. As mentioned earlier, Drew would most often wait for the offender to initiate the 'give me a break' conversation. Woman driving drunk were his prime targets. Their thinking was already impaired because of their alcoholic condition and Drew would put the fear in them after he had them in his squad car – telling them of the repercussions that they faced as a result of being arrested for drunk driving. He always checked to see if the motorist had a record. He would apply pressure to the first-time offenders – those with the least experience with the criminal justice system. With the offender in the back seat of his squad car, he would inform the law breaker of the possible consequences that they could suffer as a result of the offence that they would be charged with. Jail time, fines, lawyer's fees, and lose of driver licenses would be some of the penalties that he would outline to the arrestee. He would then wait to see if they said something to the tune of "is there some way that I can make this go away?" Drew had been very professional with the arrestee to that point but after the violator had raised the question of 'forgiveness' Drew's whole persona changed. He would exit the front seat of the car and move into the back seat with the offender. "Look lady you seem to be a good person, but you made a mistake tonight. You shouldn't have to have this drunk driving arrest follow you thought out your life," he would say to the lady. "But If I stick my neck out for you what's in it for me?" he would ask? His hand would be on the lady's leg as he asked the question. If she acquiesced to his touch he would tell her that he was going to drive to a secluded place where they could talk. He would drive his squad car to his favorite spot where he knew that the car would not be spotted. He didn't engage in much talk when they got there. He entered the back seat of the car and removed his and her garments enough so that they could have quick sex.

After his quickie with the woman, he was back in the driver's seat of the squad car. He drove back to where they started from. Drew released the woman, giving her driver's license and car keys back to her and telling her to be careful. He deduced that she was now sober enough to drive home.

PART II

Drew had left his grandmother's house and now had an apartment in a nice interracial section of town. Drew had the apartment nicely furnished and was content living by himself. He kept most of his older woman contacts from his days as an exterminator for his sexual gratification. He would visit them at their homes. He would never bring them to his dwelling. Drew had no compulsion to have an exclusive relationship with any one woman. There were two or three bars that Drew liked to patronize in different parts of the city. Drew was not a heavy drinker and he didn't go to bars to pick up women – although he was a sex addict – but he liked to watch women in the bars. He would go to a bar and sip his drink for two to three hours – just watching the women and their interactions within the bar. If he wanted sex he knew where to go, so the bar women were not lusted after. In the recess of his mind he wanted to see the women naked, but he had suppressed his old obsession of voyeurism.

Drew was enjoying his life and felt that he could exist like he was forever. He had a new car, nice apartment, made good money, dressed dapperly and had respectability. Then, one night he visited a bar in a neighborhood that he infrequently patronized. The establishment did a brisk business and on the night he chose to stop by, the place was crowded. Drew chose one of the two bar stools that were empty in the saloon and settled in for his night of sipping and watching the patrons. There was a couple next to him but shortly after Drew settled in the couple got up and left. A woman came into the bar and she occupied one of the seats vacated by the couple. She sat next to Drew. Drew could see her face through the mirror that ran the length of the bar. The mirror was behind the space that the barmaid operated in. Drew was taken aback by the beauty of the woman's face, especially her eyes. They were not big eyes, but they were rather slanted. Her eyes made her look like she had some oriental blood in her heritage. Her small mouth, just right size nose and thin lips complimented the rest of her face. Her brown skin and the texture of her hair identified her as being Black. When she stood, Drew couldn't help but gaze on her protruding behind. That behind stamped her African American heritage. She seemed real sociably as she sat down and ordered her drink from the barmaid. She and the barmaid had a running conversation for a short time while the barmaid mixed her drink. Drew was not at all bashful, but he rarely struck up conversations with people that he met in the bars. This time something compelled him to start talking to this exotic, gorgeous looking woman sitting next to him. "How's your day going?" he asked. It was a conversation starter. She answered him in a warm but unsophisticated voice. "My day's fine. What about yours?" she responded to his query with an enthusiastic smile that accentuated her exquisite face. Her speech left no doubt that she was African American. She appeared to be very outgoing and easy to talk to. From there, Drew and the woman engaged in small talk. She was unhesitant to talk about herself. Her name was Amanda. She lived in the neighborhood with her guy. "You got kids?" Drew asked. "No Baby, I don't have no children," she replied to Drew's question. She told Drew that she was 26 years old. She did not work but her guy (as she called him) took good care of her. Drew being a cop, the thought of her being a hooker flashed across Drew's mind, but he quickly dismissed that notion as he continued to talk to Amanda. She said that she liked to dance and that's why she came to this bar. According to her, the bar's dance floor and DJ were really good, and she came about

two to three times a week – just to dance. She asked Drew to
dance. Drew declined the invitation indicating that he had two
left feet when it came to dancing. While they were talking, a
patron came over and asked Amanda to dance. Amanda accepted
the invitation and left to dance with the man. Drew was
somewhat irritated when she left because he was really enjoying
communicating with her. But his irritation subsided as he
watched her on the dance floor. She had a body to go along with
that face and her movements on the dance floor were smooth and
sexy –not lurid or gaudy. As he sat watching her he felt
irresistibility drawn to her. He could hardly wait until she came
back and sat down after she was through dancing. She did come
back but he hardly commenced talking to her when another man
interrupted and asked her to dance. Drew was annoyed but he
was cool. This woman that he was enjoying interacting with did
not belong to him. He knew that he had no right to occupy her
time. At this time he wanted this woman to himself but it wasn't
going to happen. Each time she came back from dancing, another
guy would pop up and request a dance. Drew became frustrated
and after Amanda returned to her seat from her latest dance,
Drew told her, "Darling, it was nice talking to you but I got to go.
Have a nice night." He left but he did not want to go. He kept his
composure by leaving. He desired more interface with Amanda.

As he drove home, Drew thought about Amanda. She occupied
his thoughts for the next days. He reflected that he had never ever
pined for a woman before. He had to see her again. He was
determined to find out more about her. He returned to the bar in a
couple of days. He did not see her when he came in. He set down
at the bar. After a while, he was trying to figure out how he could
ask the barmaid about the woman, when Amanda walked through
the door. She was with a man. They went straight to a booth and
flopped down. Drew didn't want to be obvious, but he wanted to

look at her. He discovered that he could see the couple through the mirror behind the bar. Drew focused on Amanda through the mirror. Yes, she was as cool and beautiful as he remembered her to be when he first saw her. Amanda and the guy she was with weren't talking very much. They ordered drinks and then started dancing. They did a lot of dancing and Drew noticed that no other man asked Amanda to dance like they did when Drew first met her. The man that she was with monopolized her throughout the evening.

Drew became talkative with the barmaid. His purpose was to establish a relationship with that person so that he could do an indirect interrogation of the barmaid about Amanda. The barmaid did remember Drew from his last visit to her bar. Drew indicated that he liked the bar and that he would be coming back more often "I really like the atmosphere here," he told her. He bought another drink and tipped her generously. After a while he indicated that he was going and asked, "by the way, I think that I met that woman over there in the booth when I was here before. What's her name?" "Oh, that's Amanda and her man Billy. Sometimes she comes by herself but most often they come together," the barmaid replied to his question.

Drew became a regular at the bar and with each visit he became more obsessed with Amanda. He rarely said anything to her. A quick "hello" or "what's up" would be all that he would say as they passed each other in the bar. It appeared that Amanda remembered Drew from their first encounter because she would respond to his greetings but not enthusiastically. She was always with her man.

Drew became tight with the barmaid and he would engage her in conversations when he could. He conversed with her on various

topics – everything from the price of a drink to what was
happening in the neighborhood and the city, the latest movies and
other mundane subjects. His tips to her were excellent and she
was beginning to think that Drew might be hitting on her. Drew
had disguised his main motivation for being at the bar. His
obsession for Amanda. Drew did not let anybody in the bar know
that he was a cop. He had only asked about Amanda once before.
One night when he thought that he had the confidence of the
barmaid He asked, "What's up with that couple over there?
They're always in here but they keep to themselves. They don't
socialize." "Oh, that's Amanda and her man Billy," said the
barmaid. She had forgotten that she once told Drew who Amanda
was. Then the barmaid offered some unsolicited information
about Billy. She indicated that Billy was a small-time hustler. He
did odd jobs such as being a handyman. He could fix any
electrical problem that you might have or build you a deck, put
up a fence or sell you some weed. Drew's eyes opened wide
when the barmaid mentioned that Billy sold weed. Drew changed
the subject after that and the conversation turned to some other
topic. That night, Drew stuck around the club until closing time.
He waited until Amanda and her man left the club and he
followed out the door behind them. He wanted to see the vehicle
that the couple left the club in. It was a black pickup truck.

A couple of nights later Drew again visited the club. The black
pickup truck was in the lot when Drew arrived. Drew drove over
to the truck. Exited his vehicle and copied down the truck's
license's plate and VIN number. Drew then entered the club,
ordered a drink and got his fill of looking at Amanda. He left
after an hour or so.

The next day, at work, Drew ran the truck's license number. The
vehicle was owned by a William Bruce, a 30-year-old Black

male. Drew got the address of the owner and he ran (Billy) William Bruce's name thought the criminal justice system. Bingo! He got a hit. William Bruce had a rap sheet. He was a small-time dope dealer. He had been busted three times, mostly for selling weed. He had done a couple of short term stints in the county jail, none, no longer than 30 days. Drew wanted to run Amanda's name into the system, but he realized that he didn't know her last name. He could do that later but for now he had what he wanted. He made up his mind that he was determined to have Amanda for himself and he developed a plan to eliminate Billy from Amanda's life.

Over the next few months, Drew became very aggressive in his police work busting street dope dealers. He always knew who they were in his area of patrol, but he had not declared war on them as he now was doing. The purpose of his self-declared war on drugs was to accumulate his own stash of narcotics. He targeted cocaine dealers. It wasn't for personal use that he was accumulating this hoard of drugs. He had a diabolical purpose.

He confronted some drug dealers and took their dope. He informed them that he was giving them a break by not arresting them. "Don't let me catch you out here dealing again. I'm not arresting you but I'm gonna dump your product," he would tell them. He kept their product and added to his accrual of narcotics. By doing this, Drew made it hard on the little street dealer because they didn't have any proceeds from their drugs, but they had to explain to their higher ups how they lost the product without being arrested. As far as Drew was concerned, that was their problem. At other times, Drew would arrest a dealer and only turn in half of the product that he confiscated from the dealer as evidence for the arrest. The unreported amount would be added to his stash. A couple of small time dealers even had the nerve to try to complain to other cops about Drew. Their complaints went nowhere.

When Drew had accumulated a substantial amount of cocaine (almost a half of a kilo) he was ready to move on his plan. One night he made a visit to Billy's parked truck. He jimmied the front door lock on the truck and placed the cocaine under the driver's side front seat.

Drew didn't patrol the area that Billy lived in and he did not want to be the cop that busted Billy for drug possession. The next day at roll call, Drew took two of the cops that patrolled the area that Billy lived in aside. "Hey man, one of my snitches told me that a top dealer just got a big-time delivery of coke and it's about to hit the streets to be cut up. This snitch is pretty reliable. You ought to check it out," said Drew to his compatriots. Drew gave the officers the perpetrator's name, address and the make and model of his truck. "I would check it out myself, but I know that's you guys' territory so I'm giving it to you," Drew told the officers. They thanked him and indicated that they would follow up on the tip.

That morning the cops rolled by the address that Drew gave them, and it just happened to be the time that Billy was doing something in the back of his truck. The cops went down the street and made a U turn. They were about a half of a block down the street when Billy jumped down from the back of his truck, entered the truck cab and drove away. The cops followed him for about a couple of blocks and then put on their siren and pulled Billy over. One cop approached Billy on the driver's side and the other cop assumed the position on the passenger side. Billy was asked for his driver's license and registration. He produced them. The cops told Billy that he failed to put on his turn signal when he made a turn. The officers asked Billy could they search his vehicle Billy complied with their request. "I ain't got nothing to hide," he said. One cop took Billy to the back of the truck while the other began the search of the vehicle. It didn't take long for the cop to find the dope. Billy vehemently denied that the dope found was his. To no avail, he was arrested, jailed and charged with possession of cocaine with intent to sell. Because of the amount of cocaine found in his possession, the criminal justice system treated him as a higher up in the dope business and his bond was set accordingly – at a figure that Billy couldn't make. He was going to be in jail for a long time. He lingered in jail for 6 months before he came to trial. The prosecutor offered him a deal if he would rat out the higher ups in the dope chain, but Billy couldn't give anybody up because it wasn't his dope. Nobody believed that. He was convicted and sentenced to be incarcerated for three years.

After Billy was arrested, Drew was determined to make his move on Amanda but not too fast. Drew went to the bar every night with the hope of seeing her, but she didn't show. Drew was regularly at the bar. He came every night – still no Amanda. His frustration level grew. It was like she dropped off from the face of the earth. He knew where she lived, and he would sometimes drive by the apartment but he dared not try to go in. Had she moved? He finally got up enough nerve to ask the barmaid about Amanda "Oh, she's still in the neighborhood," the barmaid answered. "Her old man got busted. She's laying kind of low." Drew didn't ask any further questions.

Then one night shortly after Drew had entered the bar, Amanda came through the door. She didn't have the bounce and the glow that was evident on ever other occasion that Drew had observed her. She looked unkempt. Her hair was rumpled. Clothes shabbily hanging on her body like she had slept in them. She flopped into the padded both that she usually sat at and put her hand, supported by her arm, under her chin and starred at space. Drew's pulse had quickened when he saw her. She was still a knock out to Drew. He still lusted for her because she had that oriental face that had mesmerized Drew since he first laid eyes on her. Amanda didn't order a drink. She just sat there. The barmaid and the floor waitress left her alone as if they were giving her time to realize that this was a drinking establishment – they all knew about her man being busted. You could come in with your problems, but you were expected to drink while you contemplated your woes.

Drew decided to come to her rescue. He had to make his move on her. He left his seat at the bar and sauntered over to her booth. He introduced himself to her and asked, "Hey lady, can I buy you a drink?" Amanda looked up at him. Her face contoured into a half smile as she recognized him from their past encounters. "Yeah, if you want," she answered. Drew found out what she drank and went to the bar and ordered it. Upon returning to the booth with the drink Drew asked, "mind if I join you?" "No, It's alright," said Amanda. Drew went back to the bar where he had been seated, got his drink and walked coolly to join Amanda in the booth. God dam it felt good to finally be beside her. He cautioned himself – go slow. Amanda told him her name, which Drew already knew.

They drank, and Drew indicated to her that he hadn't seen her in some time. She responded that she had had a little trouble and that she hadn't been coming out. Drew didn't dig further – he knew what her problem was. He kept the conversation light. She was drinking fast, and Drew kept the drinks coming. A couple of guys came over and asked her to dance; Amanda declined. After a while Drew asked Amanda, "Where's that fellow that I always see you with?" "He's in jail," she replied. "Sorry to hear that," said a lying Drew. He didn't press her for details. After a while Amanda asked Drew, "do you drive?" "Yeah," Drew answered. "I'm a little tight and I don't have a car. Can you give me a lift?" "Sure, sure," he said. After leaving the bar, as they entered his car, he asked "where to?" as if he didn't know. She gave him the address and he steered the car to her apartment. They sat in the car and talked for a while outside her place. Drew let Amanda do most of the talking. She began to pour out her problems as the alcohol in her eased her inhibitions about spilling out her troubles. She couldn't pay the rent, her bills were going unpaid and she was even having a problem putting food on her table. She indicated that she had relied on her man to take care of her and now that he was in jail, she didn't know which way to turn. She said that she thought about whoring but that wasn't her bag. Drew asked, "you got family, don't you?" "No", she replied "I was raised in foster care." Drew listened and resisted being the knight in shining armor by offering to come to her rescue, immediately, as he wanted to do. Instead he offered to take her to dinner the next night. He got her number and indicated that he would call her before he would come to pick her up.

Drew and Amanda had their dinner date. Drew was a little awkward because he didn't have much experience at true dating. He had been over a lot of women's houses but those weren't romantic dates. He would visit a woman house to get the sex but there was no wooing involved. When he visited one of his older ladies, it was a foregone conclusion by both he and the lady that he was going to get into her pants. If they didn't want to give it up why waste his time. He was in his thirties and he had never taken a woman to a show or to dinner.

Drew did woo Amanda. They had a few dates. Drew learned a lot about this woman whom he was in love with. She was 26 years old. She told Drew that she had learned that her father was Asian, and her mother was Black. Her mother had given her up at birth and she became a ward of the State. She had been on her own since 16. Since 16, she had had a couple of relationships whereby she was the paramour of married men. She had also lived with a couple of dudes. Billy being the last one. She had been totally dependent, all of her adult existence, upon men. She had an easy-going personality, but she had no skills other than her beautiful looks and the ability to produce in men a sexual craving for her body. She had never had a job and she couldn't manage a household. The men that she was involved with, at any one time, had paid her bills. When Drew started to date her, she was behind in the rent and was about to be put out. She was not bashful about letting Drew know that she needed help. She wasn't sure about Billy's outcome because Billy had not yet been convicted. Billy had been in jail for about two months when Drew started his bonding with Amanda. Drew also let Amanda know that he was a cop. She didn't flinch one bit when he told her.

After a couple of dates, Drew took her to his apartment and he was finally able to consummate his lust for her. The sex was better than he had expected. He was able to watch her beautiful oriental like face contort to the pleasures that she received because of their intercourse. After sex, Amanda slept, and Drew scrutinized her naked body all night long. He resolved that Amanda would be his woman and he didn't need or want nobody else.

After Billy was sentenced to his three-year stretch, Amanda gave up her apartment and committed to living with Drew. She would be his woman. He would take care of her.

What about Billy? He was dumbfounded from the start of this nightmare experience. He was in jail engaged in problem solving. He scratched his brain until it was literally sore. How did this shit happen to him? One thing that he did know that was obvious to him, he had been sat up, but by who and why? He wasn't aware of any enemies that he had that hated him so much that they could perpetrate the kind of hurt that he was now in. Yeah, he had a couple of minor beefs with a couple of dudes but nothing as serious as to warrant someone setting him up to the extent that this frame up brought him. And besides the dudes that he was thinking about did not have the wherewithal to garner a half kilo of coke. He himself stayed away from messing with cocaine. He neither used it nor sold it. He had sweated a couple of guys that owed him money. One for repairing his porch steps and the other owed him money for weed. He couldn't bring himself to believe that either one of those guys could have done this to him.

Billy's whole world was turned upside down. He lost his pad, his truck, his freedom and after a while he was aware that he had lost his woman. Amanda visited him, from time to time, when he was first busted but after a while she stopped coming around. He rationalized that Amanda, being the dependent woman that she was, she had to find some man to take care of her. He thought that maybe he could get her back after he got out.

After Billy got convicted, he was sent from the county jail to the State prison. Incarceration hadn't been terribly bad up to that point. True, he had lost his freedom but life in jail was a boring routine. You ate three meals a day, you had an exercise period, you sat around and bullshitted with the other inmates and then you were locked down for the evening. You did the same dam thing every day. When he got to the State prison he expected that life would be the same as it had been in the county jail. Except that it wasn't.

When he got to the State Prison he was given a cell mate named Big Willy. Big Willy was a huge man, taller than 6 feet 5 inches and he weighed around 260 pounds. He was all muscle. Big Willy was doing a stretch for armed robbery and assault. He had been in prison about three years when Billy arrived. Nobody messed with Big Willy. He had been a gang member on the outside and he was an influential person in the joint to the rest of the prison inmate population. What Big Willy wanted – if it was possible to get for an inmate – he got it.

Billy was apprehensive when he was assigned to the cell with Big Willy, and he had reason to be. Big Willy was a touchy-feely person. He always had his hands on Billy. He would sit on the bunk with Billy and put his hand on Billy's thigh moving his hand toward Billy's crouch. He would smack Billy on the behind ever chance that he got. Those incidents pissed Billy off and his first instinct was to try and cold cock Big Willy, but he thought better of it. He was only 5 feet 8 inches and weighed 155 pounds. He knew that he was no match for Big Willy unless he had a weapon. One night, Big Willy started to rub Billy's back as they sat on the bunk talking. Billy had had enough. He jumped off the bunk and whirled around and told Big Willy, "keep your fucking hands off me." That was the end of Big Willy's attempt to finesse Billy for sex. Big Willy grabbed Billy by the throat and spun him around. "You gonna be my bitch," Big Willy announced to Billy. He tossed Billy on the bunk and flopped on top of him. Billy struggled but he was no match for the size and muscular strength of Big Willy. Big Willy told Billy that if he didn't stop struggling or if he cried out, he would eventually kill him. With his one hand on Billy's neck, Big Willy took his other hand and pulled Billy's pants down. He violated Billy by putting his penis in

Billy's anus. Billy struggled but to no avail. Big Willy hurt Billy and told him that he would continue to hurt him if Billy did not give up the struggle. There was no win in Billy's struggle. He acquiesced to Big Wiley's power and became Big Willy's hoe.

Billy suffered humiliation because, throughout the prison, it was known that he was Big Willy's "girlfriend." But being Big Willy's "lady" had its positive effect. No one else messed with Billy. Big Willy protected his piece of ass and if you disrespected Billy you were disrespecting Big Willy and Big Willy would kick your ass – even if it meant going to the Hold. Big Willy did spend time in the Hold because he would not hesitate to kick another prisoner's ass for any number of reasons. Billy always felt relief when Big Willy spent time in the Hold because it was the only time that his behind got a rest from Big Willy's enormous sexual appetite.

Despite Billy's jail house predicament, he still had a lot of time to ponder and try to figure out how he got there. He had quickly figured out that he had been set up - but by who and why. He had gone over and over in his mind everybody he knew and every situation that he had encountered that might give him a clue to who could have done it. He concluded that he could not identify anyone whom he had aggravated to the extent that someone would get to the point of framing him. He did know that it had to be someone big because small time people couldn't get hold of a half kilo of cocaine. Could it have been the cops? But he had no beef with the cops. Yes, he had been busted a couple of time selling weed but there was nothing unusual to recollect about those incidents.

Billy had lost contact with the outside world. Amanda had visited him when he was in the county jail, but she stopped coming after he was convicted. He wasn't mad at her because he figured that she had taken up with some other dude. He knew that Amanda was the type of woman that had to have a sponsor and Billy figured that she had found one.

Billy had a small circle of family, but he was not close with his kin. His mother had died a few years ago and his father had disappeared when Billy was in his early twenties. His older brother and he did not have much in common and the brother lived in another state. He did have a cousin whom he would party with and that cousin was his only visitor while he was in prison. One time when his cousin Marcus visited him Billy asked, "what happened to Amanda? You ever see her?" "Oh Yeah, she took up with a dude right after you got busted. He used to come to the bar. It turned out he was a cop. You probably remember the guy. He used to be in the bar all the time. Quiet guy. Never said much to anybody," replied Marcus. "Describe him to me," said Billy. Marcus described the man that he was talking about and Billy straight away recognized the man that Marcus portrayed. "Yeah, that dude use to sit at the bar and stare in our direction. I thought that he was a little weird, but I never paid him much attention since he never messed with no body. So he got my woman!" exclaimed Billy. "You right. He got your woman and we found out that he was a cop when he gave me a ticket one afternoon and he also ticketed another brother. The word got spread that he was a cop and after that he stopped coming to the bar. The talk on the street is that the cops sat you up and that he was involved in it and now he got your woman," Marcus volunteered that information. Upon hearing what Marcus was saying Billy's whole persona changed. He sat back in his chair. The mechanics in his brain that he had been using to solve the 'who set him up mystery' stopped ringing and twisting. They came to a rest. The mystery had been solved. Billy reasoned that there could have been only two sources that could have got hold of a half kilo of cocaine. The drug dealers or the cops. Since his dealings with the drug dealers were few and far between and he didn't owe them any money or have any beef with them, they had no motive to frame him. Yeah, he had some interaction with the cops in his past, but he was small potatoes. Why would they want to target him? This cop that now had his woman had to be the reason that his butt was sitting in the slammer. This information that Marcus was laying on him had to be the answer to his quandary. He had never considered that this dude had any role in his predicament. He had never even given this guy a thought in consideration of his problem. But, in now weighing the probability of what Marcus was saying, it had to be this guy. He was a cop. Billy had figured all along that the cops might have something to do with it and now this cop is tied to a motive. He wanted Billy's woman, and now he got her. Marcus went on and on about what else was happening on the outside, but Billy wasn't half listening. In Billy's mind the problem that he had been struggling with was solved. Though Billy hadn't had an outsider visit him since he had been in the State prison, he was glad when Marcus's visit was over. He needed time to sit back and digest the revelation that had been brought to him.

After the Marcus visit, Billy returned to his cell calm, cool and collected. He became stoic to his condition. He remained as such during the rest of his prison stay. Big Willy continued to violate him, but Billy had a new determination. He had to survive. He was going to kill that cop and he had to figure it out so that he could do so and not get caught. Scenario after scenario was played out in Billy's mind as Billy tried to develop a plan for revenge

The days, the weeks and the months went by. Billy does his time in the tense atmosphere of the prison. A prison is a place where if you don't know your place and how to act you can receive bodily harm. The strong inmates rule over the weak inmates in the penitentiary. The guards can only protect you to a certain extent and if you get on the bad side of the guards they will throw you to the wolves. You either use your brawn or you brain to safeguard yourself in jail. Billy had a protector in Big Willy – as long as Billy acceded to Big Willy's sexual dominance. But, after about a year, Big Willy's release date came, and he was gone.

Billy got a new cell mate who was a first-time convicted felon and who was not an experienced convict. Billy was then the dominate cell mate, and he ruled the cell by ensuring that both men had as much peace, as could be had in a jail cell, so that they could do their time in relative tranquility. Billy was able to control what happened inside the cell. But outside the cell, in the prison population was another matter. There were some unpleasant episodes that Billy encountered during the rest of his prison stay. Like the time there was an attempt by a couple of inmates to gang rape him in the shower because they supposed that he would be easy prey. After all, they reasoned that he had been Big Willy's pussy so they wanted a piece of him. Billy fought them off and experienced no further sexual advances after that. Also, an inmate tried to take his food, but Billy was able to stand his ground and ward off the attempt to disrespect him.

Finally, Billy's time was nearing an end. His first priority was to find a place to live once released. He began corresponding with an old girlfriend whom he had once helped. His goal was to find a place to stay when free. It was a long-shot, but it paid off. The woman didn't have anyone at the time and she knew that Billy was a hustler and that he could probably do her some good.

• • •

Billy's plan then consisted of securing some kind of income. He would pursue his handyman trade. He reasoned that he could still fix a toilet, patch a roof and lay a floor. Most of his handyman tools were lost when his truck was confiscated by the cops upon his arrest. He did have some tools that were stored in the garage of a friend. Hopefully, they would still be there.

Once his feet were economically on the ground, he would then put into action a plan to find, identify and successfully eliminate the cop that sat him up.

Eventually, Billy's time was up. He was released from prison. The woman whom he had corresponded with picked him up. She had an automobile and Billy was prepared to convince her that the use of her car would benefit him and her because he could earn money with the car in his handyman business. The woman had a job, but Billy persuaded her that he could take her back and forth to work and use the car when she was at work.

Billy wasted no time in applying efforts to procure work. In the ghetto there was always money to be made by someone who could repair a furnace, fix electrical circuits, install doors and windows or erect a fence. Billy charged much less than the going legal contractor rates for his services. It didn't take long for him to build his business to the level that he had before he was incarcerated. He just had to be careful not to get caught by the City Building Department Inspectors because he was unlicensed, and he couldn't pull any building permits, which were required by the city to ensure that the work met city specifications. His type of work was called 'jackleg' in the ghetto, which means a person who can do many different kinds of work but isn't licensed or formally schooled to do any of that work.

It took Billy about a year to bring him economically back to the level he had achieved before his imprisonment. When he was comfortable with his existence he began his **hunt.**

Billy began to engage in a hunt for the cop that sent him to prison. During the year that he had been out of jail he focused his efforts on surviving on the outside. Once he felt that had achieved his first priority of taking care of himself, he let surface his obsession that he had suppressed for the last year. Find the cop and develop a plan to waste the son-of-a-bitch.

Billy had not asked anyone about the cop who he was looking for. He had visited the bar where he and Amanda had once patronized but he saw no sign of either Amanda or the cop. Billy did not ask any questions about them. He would never ask anybody a question about this cop. Billy wanted people to think that he had no interest about his ex-old lady or her new man (the cop). He was determined to find the cop on his own.

Billy knew that the cop worked the evening shift because his cousin Marcus, when he visited him in jail, had told him that this cop had written him a ticket one evening. Billy began to stalk the police stations on the south side of the city. He would roll up on a police station during the change of shift and inconspicuously park across the street from the cop parking lot to try and spot - his cop. There were three cop stations in the area. One of them had to be the place where his cop worked out of. It took Billy longer than he expected to find his cop because he had to be unnoticeable as he tried to identify his quarry. Sometimes he parked a distant away from the cop lot and used binoculars to spy on the cops as they exited their vehicles. It was using this method that he finally spotted his prey. He had seen Drew many times in the bar when they were both patrons of that establishment. Billy still didn't know the cop's name, but he was easily recognizable. Billy had his man.

The cop got off work at midnight and Billy would sometimes be parked outside on the street when Drew would exit the parking lot to go home or where ever the hell he was going. Billy would follow the cop for a distance and then turn off. He was being cautious. He did not want the cop to have any inclination that he was being tailed. The next night that Billy tailed the cop, he would start his tail at the spot that Billy had turned off the night before. Using this method, it took Billy five nights to follow Drew to an apartment building where Billy saw Drew pull in. Billy proceeded to go past where Drew had pulled in. Billy then turned around and went back past the building. The Apartment building existed in a residential area. It was the only apartment building among a mostly single home residential neighborhood. Parking was in back of the building. Billy drove down the street and parked. He waited about a half hour and then drove back to the building. He cruised the parking spaces in the back of the building trying to identify the cop's car. He found it. It appeared that each tenant had a designated parking space because Billy saw a pole in front of each space with numbers on a sign on the poles. Billy surmised that the numbers identified each tenant's space. At the end of the parking lane there were signs that identified spaces for visitors. A fence existed about ten feet in back of the parking spaces that ran the length of the parking area. The fence separated the building from an area that contained trees, foliage and bushes. It was a small wooded area. This area ran about a half of a block and it separated the apartment building from the residential home dwellings. The apartment building was a three-floor structure with three entrances. Billy determined that there were about 36 apartments in the configuration.

• • •

Now that Billy had located the target, he returned to the building on a number of occasions to ensure that he had the lay of the land. He drove by the building both day and night. He saw tenants walk upstairs that led from the parking spaces. The stairs were not enclosed. The tenants could exit the stairs at each floor and walk to their individual apartments and enter the apartment from a porch that ran the length of the building. There was a basement but there were no apartments at that level. Upon his visits to the structure, Billy observed tenants going into the basement with bags and soap detergent. Billy took that to mean that the laundry rooms must be in the basement.

Billy cased the location for a number of weeks. His drive-bys were quick. He was being careful not to be observed. On a few occasions, at night, just before midnight, he parked his car about a block away from the building and proceeded through the wooded area that led to the fence that ran the length of the parking spaces. He lay against the fence that was in back of the parking spaces and waited for the cop to come home. The cop was like clockwork. He got off from work at midnight. He drove straight home. He would arrive at the apartment around 12:30 AM. Billy watched the cop drive into his parking space, exit his car with a small case and run up the stairs to his apartment. "I guess he can't wait to get to Amanda," Billy mumbled to himself. Billy would simulate shooting the cop by aiming his finger at the cop as if he had his gun with him. But Billy realized that a shot from that distance with a hand gun was not a sure thing. If he had a rifle, the distance would be plausible, but Billy did not have a rifle. And furthermore, Billy did not plan on killing the cop from a distant. He wanted to be up close and personal when he blew the cop away. Besides Billy had one more step in his plan to eliminate the cop.

• • •

Billy visited the west side of Chicago. He was bar hoping. In jail, he remembered that there were a number of bars that his cell mate, Big Willy, had mentioned that he frequented. Billy was looking for Big Willy. He was frustrated when he was unable to locate the object of his search after visiting a number of bars during a three-week period. But, Billy was persistent. He kept up the hunt without asking anybody at the bars that he visited if they knew Big Willy. He would walk into a bar, give the bar a quick perusal and move on. Finally, after about a month of searching and multiple visits to some of the bars, Billy walked into a bar on west Madison Street and there was Big Willy – shooting pool. Billy instantly left the bar and went back to his car. He did not want to be seen talking to Big Willy. Billy waited until a car, which was in front of the bar, drive off and then Billy moved into that space in front of the bar. He waited for Big Willy to leave. Big Willy exited the bar about an hour later. Billy beckoned to Big Willy from inside his car. Big Willy stopped and bent over to look in the car when he heard his name. After a moment he recognized Billy. "What the fuck you want?" asked Big Willy. He was apprehensive after he recognized Billy. After all, this was the mark that he raped in jail. Billy had slid over to the passenger side of his car and he quickly sought to calm any fears that Big Willy might have. "Look," said Billy, "I got this dude who will be carrying a large sum of cash money and he can be had but he's a big dude and I need some muscle to take him down. I know that he will be carrying about 20 or 30 grand. Get in and I can lay it out to you," Billy indicated. Billy slid back over to the driver's side. Big Willy, still apprehensive, opened the car door and slid in. Billy kept his hands on the wheel in an effort to allay any fears that Big Willy might have of an ambush.

Billy began telling Big Willy the details of the plan. "I know of this dude who is a courier for the Mexican Mafia. He collects drug money from the south side drug dealers that are supplied by the Mexican Mafia. He collects once a week and then turns over the money to the people that he works for. Every Tuesday he spends all day collecting the dough. He takes it home at night and then the next day he turns the money over to the Mexicans. He carries the cash in a case that he has with him as he makes his rounds He's like clockwork. Every Tuesday he's flush with cash. I want that money but as I said he's a big dude. And I need someone like you to help me take him down." Big Willy asked, "How you know about this dude?" "You know that I was in the business. That's what I was doing time for," said Billy. "But you said that you was innocent," replied Big Willy. "Yeah, yeah. What con don't say they was innocent? I was in the business up to my neck. How you think that I got caught with a half kilo of cane?"

Big Willy grilled Billy about the caper. "How you plan to take the dude down?" he asked. "He probably is carrying a gat," Big Willy predicted. "Yeah, that's why we have to take him hard and fast and that's why I need you," said Billy. "Look," continued Billy, "I'll take you by the place where we going to take him down." Billy drove to the south side apartment of the target and showed Big Willy the layout. They slowly drove down the driveway of the apartment building and Billy pointed out the parking space, the stairs and the basement where they would be in hiding and waiting for the mark to enter the stairs. "We jump him real quick and beat the shit out of him and then grab the case. We got to hurt him bad so that he don't follow us. We gonna come in from across the fence that you see there." Billy pointed out the fence to Big Willy. "We gonna leave the same way." Billy also drove to the spot where they would park the car in back of the wooded area that led to the fence.

"Looks like you got it all planned out," said Big Willy enthusiastically. He had bought into Billy's plan. He had only one more question. "You sure the dude's gonna have that kind of money on him?" asked Big Willy. "He been the courier for years. He's like clockwork. We gonna take him down," said Billy.

It was Sunday when Billy and Big Willy cased the hit. Billy drove Big Willy back to the West side and told Big Willy that he would pick him up on the corner of Madison and California at 9:30 PM sharp on Tuesday of that week. He cautioned Big Willy not to mention the job to anyone. "We don't want the Mexican Mafia coming after us because some bastard shot his mouth off. And don't be late. We need to be in place at the fence at about 11:30," said Billy. Big Willy jumped out the car and came around to the driver's side and gave Billy a high five. "Don't worry I'll be on time and I'll kept my mouth shut," said Big Willy as he backed away from the car.

Billy drove back to the south side with nervous anticipation in his stomach. His plan was laid out. There was nothing more that Billy could do. There was no sense in stressing about. It would either work or not. Billy was committed to doing it and willing to suffer the consequence if it failed but he was confident that it would not fail.

The next day, Monday was the slowest day of Billy's life. He wished that he had set the day for Monday instead of Tuesday. It had been two years since he had been released from prison. He had spent time getting back on his feet economically. He had found the cop that framed him, located where he lived, developed a plan to kill him and now it was time to execute that plan. He was experiencing a sensation of taking in deep breaths and sucking in air that he had never experienced in his life. He diagnosed that as nerves and anticipation. He had to calm his nerves. He knew that he could only pull this thing off if he remained cool and collected.

When Tuesday did come, Billy forced himself to calm down, relax and be his normal self. He ate a good breakfast, busied himself all day by repairing a roof for one of his customers and cleaned and loaded his gun before he ate dinner in the evening. Billy had set 9:30 PM as the time that he would pick up Big Willy on the west side. After dinner he killed some time at a local bar nursing a couple of drinks and shooting the breeze with the bar customers as he would normally do. At quarter after eight he was out of the bar and on his way to the west side.

Big Willey was at the corner at the appointed time. As he jumped into the car Billy drove away and began to go over the plan. "We get to the fence at 11:15 and lay flat until 11:45. At that time, we cross the fence and go to the basement steps. We'll be hiding in the basement well. Our man usually comes in at after 12.15. When he gets out of his car and hits the first step, I'll come from the left side of the basement stairway and you come from the right side I'll hit his legs with a stick and you got to lay some heavy blows on him quickly. You got to knock the mother fucker senseless. If he has a gun, I'll get it and I'll grab the case and we'll be out of there and back across the fence. He's got to be hurt so bad that he can't even think about trying to come after us. You got that?" Billy asked. "Sure, sure," Big Wiley answered. "Just concentrate and in a couple of hours we'll have 20 to 30 grand," said Billy.

It took about an hour to drive from the west side to the south side. Billy stayed off of the expressway. He took the street which took a little longer. They had plenty of time. They arrived at the place where they would park the car just off the wooded area that led to the fence where they would hide. They were a little earlier then had been intended. They sat in the car until 11:10 PM and then left the car to cross the wooded area that led to the fence. As they approached the fence, Billy looked up into a blackened sky. It was a warm night. No moonlight was showing. It smelled like rain. There was probably a cloud cover overhead. It was perfect for Billy's intended purpose. The only light for the area was the light that illuminated the parking spaces. They arrived at the fence at 11:15 and lay down as planned. During the time that they lay at the fence, a couple of cars entered the parking spaces away from their target area and the occupants exited the cars and went up the stairs to their apartments. All of a sudden Billy realized that his plan was flawed. Every time that he had cased the job, the cop drove up and was the only car coming into the spaces. What if another car or cars were to enter the parking spaces at the same time that the cop entered his space? What would he do? Would he have to abort the plan? He decided that it was too late to change the plan. He would have to let it play out.

At 11:55 he and Big Willy jumped the fence and ran to the basement stairs. They were now in place. Billy with his stick (and his gun) and Big Willy with his fists. Billy could hear his heart pound as they waited for the time to pass. 12 midnight came. Billy expected the cop to come anywhere from 12:10 to 12:20. 12:15 passed – no car entered the parking spaces. 12:30 came and went. No cop. Billy cursed to himself, "this bastard would have to be late for his own funeral." Billy was about to go to the other side of the stairs to ensure that Big Willy was remaining calm when lights appeared in the driveway that led to the parking spaces. As the car came down the driveway, Billy recognized the head lights. It was his target car. The cop was finally here to get his due. Billy crouched like a stalking tiger as the cop pulled into his parking space. The car trunk popped open and the cop exited the car and went to the rear to get something from the trunk. It appeared to be dry cleaning wrapped in a plastic bag. He slammed the trunk and began walking towards the steps where Billy and Big Willy were hidden in ambush. As the cop put his foot on the first step, Billy fired between the slats from beneath the steps into the cop's groin. The cop spun around and fell to the ground and Billy was out from under the steps moments after the cop hit the ground. He stood over the withering cop, looked him in the eye and then fired a bullet into his head. Big Willy popped up from his hiding place in the stair well and said to Billy, "you didn't say anything about shooting the fucker." Billy commanded Big Willy, "get the god damn money case." As Big Willy went for the case, Billy went for the cop's gun. Big Willy got the case and as he opened it he proclaimed, "hey, there ain't no money in here." Those were the last words that Big Willy uttered. Billy shot him in the head with the cop's gun. "Rape that," Billy said as he snuffed Big Willy's life out. Billy threw the cop's gun down and placed his gun in Big Willy's, hand and fired the weapon. This was the gun that Billy used to shoot the cop. He wanted Big Willy's prints on the gun and gunshot residue on Big Willy's hand.

The whole operation took less than three minutes. After firing the gun in Big Willy's hand, Billy collected the stick that he had brought with him and sprinted for the fence. Once over the fence, he sprawled flat on his stomach He took a little time to try and erase evidence that two men had been lying in wait on the ground. Using the stick that he had carried with him he quietly swished the area in an effort to remove any evidence that there were two person's foot prints on the ground. He then began crawling to the wooded area and turned over, in a flat position on his back, to look back at the apartment complex. He saw that lights had popped on in the apartments above the parking spaces. The tenants were responding to the gun fire that they had heard. Tenants were also coming out on to the porches. Billy viewed the people on the balconies looking down, pointing and yelling toward the two men lying prone on the ground. They were not looking in his direction. Billy was now in the wooded area, but he kept low to the ground as to not attract any attention from those tenants who might look in his direction. The dark clouded night helped to conceal him as he crawled the last few feet to his car. He crawled to the driver's side of his car, opened the door, boosted himself into the driver's seat and stuck his key in the ignition. Billy drove away with the car lights off for about a block before he turned them on. As he was leaving the area he heard sirens. He thought, 'It didn't take the cops long to respond.'

Billy went home, cleaned up and went to bed. He couldn't sleep. He wanted to have his night to be normal, as any other night had been, but adrenaline was still flowing, and he couldn't bring it down. Maybe, if he screwed his woman he could go to sleep. It usually knocked him out. He woke his woman and laid one on her, but it didn't work. After having sex, he was still wide awake. He left the bedroom and sacked out on the coach in the living room. He turned on the television and began to flip through channels. He watched a couple of programs and finally dozed off but about 4:30 in the morning He was awaken by a morning news flash on the TV "Breaking story, breaking story. Two men shot dead on the south side of Chicago. More news to come," was the announcement that came from the TV. Billy sat up on the couch and then went to the kitchen and poured himself a bowl of cereal. He returned to the coach and directed his full attention to the news that was coming from the television.

More details of the shooting were being broadcasted. The channel had a reporter on the scene who was reporting that one of the dead men was a police officer. She had the camera pan the scene in back of her to show the numerous police present at the scene and she was trying to get a police spokesman to come on camera to give details of the shooting, but the cops only confirmed that one of the victims was an off-duty police officer.

Over the next hours and days of reporting, the media began to get the facts from the police. They said that it was an attempted robbery that had gone bad. The perpetrator was identified as William "Big Willy" Turner, and his picture was plastered over the TV stations and the newspapers. The cop's name was Drew Harrison and he was being treated as a hero – as all cops who die from gun play are treated. Amanda was identified as the dead cop's betrothed. All the cop awards that Officer Harrison had won were mentioned. The papers theorized that Willy Turner had picked Drew Harrison to rob at random but did not know that he had picked a cop as his victim. A shootout occurred and both men shot each other dead.

Billy, with selfish interest, followed every aspect of the story with gleeful pride in that his planning had successfully pulled off his revenge for the cop who had set him up to go to prison and the man who had took his manhood while he was in jail. The cops considered the case closed.

After his escapade, Billy went on to lead a mundane life. He did nothing for the rest of his life that involved breaking the law except to occasionally get a traffic ticket. He never again used or sold drugs. He had a criminal record that he could do nothing about in a legal sense, because of the felony drug bust that sent him to jail, and which embarked him on the adventure that led him to murder two men who in his mind deserved to die. Also, in his mind, he had expunged his own record and satisfied his individual sense of justice. He even felt some sense of accomplishment and payback for every wrongfully committed act by the police that lead to the prosecution, incarceration, injury, death or disrespect of Black people. He never tried to get Amanda back. He did not want to have anything to do with something that could ever tie him to the murders that he had committed.